D0064757

FLASH POINT

Flash Point

M. S. CRAIG

Dodd, Mead & Company

NEW YORK

Published by
Dodd, Mead & Company, Inc.
79 Madison Avenue, New York, N.Y. 10016
Distributed in Canada by
McClelland and Stewart Limited, Toronto
Manufactured in the United States of America

First Edition

1 2 3 4 5 6 7 8 9 10

Library of Congress Cataloging-in-Publication Data

Craig, M. S.
    Flash point.

    I. Title.
PS3553.R226F53 1987   813'.54   86-11637
ISBN 0-396-08884-8

For Dan
with love and gratitude
for the gift of his mountain

Chapter 1

Although Luke Adams had been away from California a third of his life, he didn't give the changing landscape north of San Francisco a second glance. Instead, he pressed his rented car steadily against both the miles and the speed limit. Fear made a man single-minded. He had been deeply concerned to hear that the man who raised him, Ash Porter, had been left crippled by a nearly fatal accident. Ash himself had turned that concern to fear with his last letter. It was crazy enough for an old man in a wheelchair to try to make it alone in a mountain cabin. To try that with an arsonist loose on the west slopes of the Sierras was pushing past risk toward suicide.

It was hard to believe that Ash had even tried to keep him from coming home.

"Another time," Ash had written. "Almost any other time. Things are clean out of hand here. I can't go into it all, but a firebug is loose on this mountain. I know you remember Jerry Hodges. He's been hauling as an independent. Somebody rigged his truck and blew him to bits. Never had a chance. It's a wonder he's the only one, what with a loaded gun inside every cabin door. I appreciate your wanting to check up on me after what happened. You know I'd rather see you than any man alive, but not now, son. Anytime but now."

Talk about laying a trip on somebody. Here was a guy who had taken Luke in as an orphaned kid, shoved him through high school, and then sent him off with a stake. He would have to be some kind of an ingrate to let a firebug keep him away. And somebody had to knock some sense into the old man. For Ash even to think about staying up there alone was ridiculous. Luke had put in for leave the day he got that letter.

He fretted the car across the Richmond Bridge and through the city to head north again. Now that he was nearing the old man's home in the Sierras, the miles couldn't pass fast enough. Either the valley road stretched longer than he recalled, or impatience was distorting his memory.

The last town on the valley floor was Featherton. Just beyond the lumber-scaling station, he made a right turn onto the mountain road. Almost at once the air blew in cooler, fragrant with the smell of the woods. The incline was steep, and Luke held the rented car to an easy fifty-five miles an hour and gave himself looking time. Good looking time. The west slope of the Sierras still belonged to him, as comfortable and familiar as the lines of his own square jaw.

It had been a long trip from Germany and an expensive one, but only a few miles of mountain road lay between him and Ash now. Ash used to tell him the mountains were layered in three ways, by the weather, the trees that grew there, and the people who settled in to stay. The first level of the mountain, called the Digger Pine Belt, edged up from the valley heat. Although it was more built up than Luke remembered, the sense of the area was the same: small fenced acreages that the mountain people called "the suburbs," and a scattering of run-down farms without enough dirt between the stones to scratch a living from.

He had forgotten how well they maintained those mountain roads, but then, they had to. This was lumbering country. A loaded logging truck could weigh thirty-seven tons, more than enough to chew up an ordinary highway without anyone's even noticing it was caught in the teeth of its tire treads.

When the road had wound up above the 2,500-foot level, the trees began thrusting higher into the afternoon sunlight, ponderosa pine and cedar, broken up by stands of Douglas fir. Luke grinned to himself. This was his kind of mountain, homesteading country, with close little communities like Bardenville and Madrone that lay just a few miles down the mountain from Ash's place.

With the whole Sierra slope to choose from, the Indians had chosen this yellow pine belt to settle into. They'd stayed through one fight after another ever since. Maybe fighting came with the altitude. Gold prospectors had scrapped over claims and settlers for their homesteads. As a boy Luke had listened to bitter wrangling between the powerful lumber corporations and the independent operators like Ash Porter. He had even filled his own slot in the endemic rivalry between the valley people and those on the mountain. Above 3,500 feet the winters came too harsh for anybody but loggers and hardrock miners, but this part of the mountain was sweet—good weather, growing earth, and streams bright with trout.

He had barely passed the turnoff toward Madrone when the vibration shuddered through his rental car.

For a split second Luke's mind registered earthquake. Natural response. The ghosts of California's restless faults haunted the nightmares of any kid who grew up here. The blast trembled the air before he eased the car to a stop at the edge of the road. The reflection in the side-view mirror was white, dense smoke billowing up from the mountain slope behind him.

Not earthquake, but explosion, followed by fire.

The burgeoning pillar rose, folding in on itself, cresting the tops of the trees and fanning out to belly into a widening shroud over the gray-green of Douglas firs. Already the pungency of evergreen was overwhelmed by the stench of burning rubber.

He groaned, remembering Ash's words: "Not now, son. Anytime but now."

Shouts filtered through the woods as a siren wailed from the valley below. Pocketing the car keys, he followed scent and sound, startled to realize he had lost the knack of running swiftly over a littered forest floor. A spicy scent like witch hazel mingled with the smoke as he ran through the brush thick with the weed he knew only as mountain misery.

The tower of flame was visible through the trees before he reached the clearing. People were running and shouting, scattering in all directions. A building, totally enveloped in leaping tongues of fire, crackled and hooted, its heat scorching against his face. A woman was screaming, a high-pitched scream that faltered, found wind, and rose again. Around the blazing building a line of men were digging a fire line to cut off its spread. He came out of the woods behind Maude's Place, where a line of men with shovels were already hacking at the earth. Garden hoses snaked in tortured spirals from the feed store and the sides of the houses along the street. A couple of them pumped steady streams into the gaping side of what Luke remembered as being an old, broken-down garage.

As he shielded his face against the blasts of heat, he saw a soaked and shrouded figure stagger out of the blazing building, crouching like an ox in harness from the weight of the limp body he was dragging behind him.

Ten years of soldiering sharpens anyone's reflexes. Luke had circled Maude's line of garbage cans and had a sharpshooter spade in his hands by the time they got that still-smoking body bundled across the street and into Maude's Place.

In the frenzied hour that followed, he registered only glimpses of the chaos around him. Along with five or six others, he began to dig, tossing the earth onto fresh fires that bloomed along the edge of the woods. The heat from the burning garage and the sweat of his efforts glued falling sparks to his skin. Luke cursed to himself. He could deal with pain, but it made him mad as hell, and fire scared him spitless. Why in the devil hadn't he just driven right on by and gone straight up the mountain to Ash's, where he wanted to be?

A fire truck finally got there, and then another, followed by a sheriff's car whose siren kept screaming, adding its decibel count to the thunder of falling timbers and men's shouting voices.

Finally it was all but over. Flames no longer leaped from the smoking ashes of the garage. The road was crowded with exhausted fire fighters and gapers whose cars were lined up clear out to the highway. A burly man in an open-necked sheriff's shirt circled the ruin, listening and nodding. When he turned, Luke did a double take. Eddie Dodge! He hadn't thought of Dodge twice since high school. Eddie was nodding and frowning as he scratched notes in a spiral pad.

Luke had probably fought with Eddie Dodge more times during those four years than he had with any other single human being in his whole life. It hadn't been anything he chose. You either let the valley kids beat you down with their mouths or you gave it back to them with your fists. He hadn't won all those fights, but neither had he lost more than his share. A kid who's only a twist of wiry muscle has an odds-even chance against a big guy who carries a lot of lard. But Luke had made some cold trips back up the mountain

5

on that school bus because of Eddie Dodge. Luke washed Eddie's blood and his own out of his shirt more than once to shiver home dripping wet rather than face Ash after another fight.

All of the garage except the studs and a part of the folded roof had been consumed or had fallen away. Inside that black skeleton the smoldering chassis of a burned car breathed mingled smoke and steam against the background of scorched trees. A few men with blackened faces still fed desultory streams of water onto the smoking ashes.

Madrone hadn't changed much from what he remembered. Maude's restaurant, the feed store that carried every kind of hardware except what you needed, the gas station with a couple of shelves of dusty emergency groceries and a refrigerator case filled with drinkables and butter, five or six houses, and this burned-out hulk along with a scattering of barns set back in the woods.

Eddie came over, planting himself solidly to stare into Luke's face.

"Do I know you?" he asked.

"You used to. Luke Adams."

Dodge frowned before grinning broadly. Close up, the sheriff's badge showed "Deputy." That figured. The mountains never got more than a deputy, and like Dodge, these were usually guys from the valley appointed by the county sheriff to deal with people they knew nothing about. "Good God. Luke Adams. Haven't thought of you in years." He looked him up and down. "You've sure filled out."

Luke was perversely tempted to focus on Eddie's sagging belly and return the compliment.

"Where'd you come from?" Dodge went on.

Luke wagged his head toward the road. "I was driving up the mountain when I felt the explosion. I cut through the woods."

6

Eddie shook his head. "No. I mean how come you're here? I thought you went army."

"I did. I'm on leave. I was on my way up to see Ash."

Eddie took a minute to absorb this. "That's right, sure. He raised you, didn't he? After your mom . . ." Luke could almost watch him fitting the pieces in place under that thatch of sweat-darkened pale hair. Eddie frowned. "Tough about Porter's accident." He paused. "God only knows how he's managing up there all alone, in a wheelchair and all. How's he getting along?"

"I was on my way up there to see," Luke told him.

"That's right. That's what you said. See anybody in the woods?" he went on. "Maybe a man running?"

"A lot of people were running when I broke through the woods."

"Nobody in particular?"

Luke shook his head.

"You'll be around if I need to talk to you. At Ash's place?"

"Sure, Eddie," he said.

"Just in case," Dodge added. Clearly he had been watching cop programs on TV. He had both the phrases and the tone of vague threat honed to a fine edge of insinuation.

The crowd had thinned out. Luke studied faces, looking for somebody else he knew. He saw Maude come out on the porch of her restaurant and go back in, but she didn't notice him. The sense of belonging that had grown steadily through the drive up from the valley had deserted him. He was only a curious stranger caught in a tragedy he couldn't feel. Slender, wide-shouldered men in faded jeans stared at the dying fire, their faces ridged with concern. Women had the luxury of tears; a few sobbed quietly, but most of them stood silent and tearstained, standing close to their men, some with wide-eyed children braced on one hip. Their talk

7

was subdued, whispery with the caution of the living in the presence of the known dead. Luke heard the phrase "Nan's boy" without being able to put a face to it. He felt people's eyes on him, narrowed by curiosity.

Then he saw Burt Roberts, who had come in as resident manager for Larson and Frane Lumber Company when Luke was growing up. It was astonishing how little ten years could change a man. Roberts had that kind of take-charge face that aged well. His presence wasn't hurt by the way he was dressed, either. It was hard for a first sergeant in the army to justify the cost of civilian clothes, but Luke had priced camel-hair blazers like the smoke-streaked one over Roberts's arm. Roberts wasn't hurting for money to dress like that. But power and money always hung out together. Luke didn't recognize the people standing with Roberts—a man who looked to be about Luke's age and a slender blond girl in riding pants.

Finally, thank God, it was over and he could get up to Ash's, where he belonged. He knew for sure that Ash had been wondering what happened to him for a good half-hour. Ash would have seen the first wisp of smoke from the fire with those binoculars of his. By now he was probably turning the air blue with the fury of his helpless concern.

Luke hesitated. No path led through those woods. He was safer going out to the road and following it until he got to the car. Once there, he sat a moment, perfectly still. He had eaten dinner with Ash's daughter Linden in San Francisco the night before. The evening had been wholly unsatisfactory. Not only had Linden shown a callous lack of interest in her father's safety, she had also dismissed the arson on the mountain by mouthing clichés about feuds. There was enough danger of fire on the mountain without human mischief. Even with the good luck of late-August rains, September could still see low flash points. A man couldn't grow up on that mountain without getting his consciousness raised. When the temperature was high and the humidity low enough, a pine didn't need more than a carbon spark from the exhaust of a car to flash into fire. He could remember whole months when the gauges outside the forest-service office hung on red and cars weren't even allowed to drive through the forests. Trees are wood and wood is fuel and Bambi wasn't the first or the last to get his that way.

Ash had said in his letter that Jerry Hodges had been blown up in his truck. Luke remembered Hodges. Although Jerry was closer to Luke's age than Ash's, he and the old man had been friends. Luke had halfway worshiped Hodges through grade school, when Jerry had been a star tackle in high school. But instead of college, he'd gone into lumbering, like his dad before him.

Both Jerry's dad and Porter had done the one job in lumbering that even impressed a cocky kid. They were "fallers," the Samsons who walked into the woods to bring down giants. Not many fallers lived to be old men. In Placer's, the roughest tavern in Bardenville, one whole wall was hung with the boots of dead fallers. It was tough, dangerous, lonely work. Fallers preferred to go into the woods alone, knowing how many places death could wait for them. To watch a good faller work, even from the distance Ash always banished Luke to, was to be privy to magic. One man bringing down a single tree within an inch of where he wanted it to go. When it struck the earth, the heart of the mountain missed a beat. But not until that tree struck could the faller be sure that a widow-maker wasn't up there with his name on it. Giant limbs or the lopped-off top of the tree, invisible through the dense needles, fell straight down, driving the faller into the earth.

Before Luke could pull back onto the road, a logging

truck roared round the curve ahead to thunder past. The car swayed giddily from the draft. Kid rules. Look up the mountain and then feel the ground before you cross the road. Even when the driver wasn't giving the gas pedal the benefit of his total body weight, the hurtling gravity of those logging trucks loaded with swaying tree trunks had defined deadly force for Luke before he ever heard the phrase.

The inside of his car reeked with the stench of smoke. He wished he didn't keep hearing the sound of women crying.

The only time he had been back after finishing high school he had come to admit to Ash that he wasn't making it out in the world and was going to go army. "Fighting's never paid off very well for you," Ash reminded him.

Luke had been young enough then to color up at his words. "I'm not a hotheaded kid anymore, Ash. If I'm going to make it on my own, I need training. The army's the only easy way to get that."

"Anything that puts you into a fight is the hard way, Luke Adams."

So much for trying to tell a twenty-year-old anything. Anyway, it had been too late. He had already signed on.

Not much had changed that first time. Ash's daughter Linden was still on the mountain, living with Ash and working for Burt Roberts at the office of Larson and Frane, who owned most of the timberland around there except what the government held. Ash didn't like his daughter's working for Roberts, but that wasn't surprising. Small operators hated the big companies on principle. When government contracts came up, the little guys didn't have a chance. Whether the contracts were for salvage or live lumber, the corporations could bid over market price, gambling that inflation would catch up with them. That squeezed everyone else out. And the company's hiring rankled. With local foresters out of work, they brought in young guys from outside.

Ash had kept him up on the news from home by letter. Sometimes he even sent the local paper. Luke always meant to get back, but something always came up. None of his Stateside furloughs sounded long enough to justify the cost of a quick trip back home. Then he was in Germany and drunk with the novelty of Europe. Luke sent Ash a cuckoo clock from Germany and binoculars from Switzerland. That man would rather spot a new bird than get a royal flush. Ash's letters kept coming, and sometimes Luke almost wore them out. Ash wrote about new birds he'd sighted, who'd gotten married, and who had bought a new pickup truck.

The personal news was always down at the end and tersely stated. In one letter Ash wrote, "Linden and I had one scrap too many. She packed out of here and is down in San Francisco, working for God knows who."

He wrote Ash it was natural for a grown kid to want to leave home, even a girl. "You raise kids up and they take off. I did, didn't I?"

Ash didn't mention Linden's leaving again except to say that Luke's going off had been different: He and Ash had parted as friends.

Since Ash didn't write like clockwork, Luke didn't realize when the letters stopped. That was May and a lot was going on. June came and then July, with still no word from Ash. Luke felt edgy about it and tried to tell himself that Ash just got tired of scratching "APO" on envelopes a couple of times a month. After all, by that time he had been doing it for ten years.

Luke kept in touch on his end anyway, ragging at Ash a little about getting lazy in his old age. The day the letter came from Ash, Luke put in for a month's emergency leave. The old man had been in an accident.

Ash was stingy with details, only saying that one of Larson and Frane's lumber trucks went out of control and sideswiped him before jackknifing on the road right above Madrone. After doing all they could with surgery and therapy, they had shipped him back home in a wheelchair. "Don't take it hard," Ash told him. "I tell myself I've probably done my share of walking already."

Luke *did* take it hard. Approval of his leave came through the day after a car bomb killed one airman and another one's wife and injured some twenty people at the Rhein-Main Air Base in Frankfurt. He started waking up sweaty, waiting for the days to pass. Ash was all the family he remembered, and probably more than he deserved considering what a heller he'd been in high school.

That last letter from Ash arrived when Luke was already packing. Because Ash had been so explicit about his not coming home, Luke didn't write him his plans. Instead, he called that morning just before leaving San Francisco. Ash shouted at him over the phone. "You never did half learn to mind. I tell you, Luke, you don't want to come up here the way things are. What kind of a soldier are you, anyway? Whoop it up down there in the city and have a helluva good time. That's what military leaves are all about."

Luke told him to put an extra potato in the soup and tie up the dog. Ash was still ranting when Luke hung up the phone.

The general store was already lit against the coming darkness. Luke strained to see the figure planted behind the cash register. So Ruby was still running the store. He slowed going past Burt Roberts's place. The house, with the local office of Larson and Frane built off to the left, still looked good, substantial behind its circle drive. To the right of the house Roberts had added stables, a long line of them, with corrals and pens. The last section was built up, with something like a carriage house on top with windows and a weather vane. The hanging wooden sign at the drive's entrance bore the silhouette of a prancing horse and the single word "AMIE."

Only two miles more to home. Luke gave the car a boost of extra gas, as excited as a kid at the thought of seeing Ash again. Never mind the father he never knew and the mother who was a fading voice. Ash was family.

The familiar drive wound past the Porter mailbox and meandered into a clearing past a line of second-growth ponderosa pine. In spite of the disappointing evening with Linden, he was glad she had warned him that the place would look different. Ten years before, Ash's house and the cabin across the lot had nestled in a grove of Douglas firs. The big trees were now gone, leaving both buildings standing in what was al- most a clearing unless you counted the second-growth shrub, mostly manzanita that was growing between the stumps. Bandit, the dog who roared down the drive toward the car, was big and dark, with an obvious decision-making problem. His tail was wagging as vi- olently as he was barking. At least Ash would know he had finally gotten there.

Ash had always called the place a cabin, but it was so much more than that: cedar shingles, a deep-pitched roof, and a chimney darkened by fragrant fires. Wooden tubs still spilled scarlet-and-white petunias onto the battleship-gray paint of the porch. Starting those seeds had been one of Luke's childhood chores. Beyond that a giant stand of sunflowers gaped slavishly toward the giant trees blocking the last light of the sun. The double-staggered row of beehives had been moved closer to the rental cabin. Shaded by the giant leaves of castor plants, they wandered down the slope between the big house and the second cabin. Ash had written, two or three years before, that he had been "careless and earned a good stinging. I'm sensitized now. I'd get the things off the place if I didn't like watching them so much." The little cabin Ash kept rented out showed its years. The roof with its burden of fallen fir needles seemed to be wholly supported by the blooming vine on the drainpipe.

The dog's tail won. By the time Luke reached the porch, his hands were slick with saliva and only a rapid right to the animal's chest had saved him from a face-washing. Luke noticed the wooden ramp that had been added at the end of the stairs. At least Ash was able to go in and out of the house without assistance.

A tantalizing scent of browned beef poured through the open door as he mounted the stairs. "Luke," Ash called from inside. "Shove that critter away and get in here." A lamp bloomed in the dark room as he pushed the door open.

He was prepared to see Ash in a wheelchair, but not looking the way he did. Time, along with the accident, had reduced him to a small curl of a body nestled between cushions. Only his arms were still full-sized, still swelling with muscle.

This had been a man who had felled Douglas firs all alone, as Luke, banished to a point well beyond danger, had waited to clap his hands to his ears at the thunder of a giant's fall.

Once Ash's hair had been as black as Linden's. Now it was mingled gray and white and almost shoulder-length. Ash's rough hands, callused from the wheels, held Luke's shoulders tight for a painful moment. The old man's eyes were as clear and blue as the noon sky in winter. "God, it's good to see you, Luke," he said angrily. "But I told you to stay away. I made that clear!"

"So I never half minded," Luke told him. The old man's hair smelled like the rough-cut Durham he always smoked. Home.

"Come into the light where I can see you," Ash ordered.

The library table under the window was cluttered with books of all sizes. The copy of *Birds of the West* was noticeably shabby. Beside it lay the binoculars Luke had priced in horror and come back twice to finger before he had let go of the money and had them sent to him.

"See how much time has passed?" Ash complained. "I don't know whether you want coffee or whiskey."

Luke laughed. "Whiskey. I want to see if yours still tastes as much like furniture polish as it did when I sneaked it as a kid. But that's only if you join me," he added hastily.

"Little rotter." Ash grinned, wheeling toward the yellow oak washstand where he had always stored his hooch. "After that, we'll eat. If you can't smell that pot roast, you have a helluva cold."

Luke knew better than to protest being waited on. And to tell the truth, he was impressed by how well the old man was managing this small world of his. But too many dangers surrounded this tailored cocoon. "I don't deserve this kind of welcome after you told me not to come."

Ash snorted. "If you had done what I told you, I would have known you for an impostor." He poured a double shot of Teacher's Scotch and looked up. "Rocks?" he asked.

"Rocks are fine."

With his back turned, Ash clawed ice from a freezer bin in the kitchen just off the front room. The refrigerator was new, as was the square modern gas stove where the old range had stood. Luke studied it thoughtfully. Propane gas had to be delivered fairly regularly.

The driver would be one more person keeping an eye out that Ash was functioning. The stove had a fire burner on the end that would hold enough wood to take the chill off the house. Somebody had to keep that box filled with lengths of cedar wood. "I don't know why you had to come back while all this hulla-balloo is going on. You didn't see Linden, did you, on the way up?"

"She bought me dinner last night. She looks great."

"I guess she told you she never comes home."

"I got that impression," Luke admitted.

Ash sat without moving for a moment, his back still to Luke. "Regret pays no bills, but I rue that Linden didn't take off right after high school like you did. We might be better friends now if she had."

Cryptic. Luke throttled back a dozen questions that were none of his business. When he went away to the army, Linden had been queen of her world. She was luminously happy, loving her job, loving her life. As a twenty-year-old still tingling from the indignities of adolescence, he had been jealous as hell of that girl. Even the unfair way she treated him when Ash wasn't around hadn't diminished his awe of her. What had happened to Linden up here on this mountain? What catalyst had turned a bright, warm girl into a sleek, brisk woman, bitter against her own kind?

Ash handed Luke his drink and touched his own glass against the rim. "I swore I wouldn't bother you about the fire until after supper, but it looks like you got into it for yourself." He nodded at Luke's stained shirt. "It looked fast and dirty from here. What went up?"

"That old garage across the street from Maude's Place in Madrone," Luke told him. "When it blew up, I was on the road above. When I got there everybody in town was fighting it. Finally the fire truck came . . ."

Ash listened intently, frowning. Suddenly he broke in. "Today isn't Saturday, is it?"

"Sure it is."

Ash turned away, drawing a deep breath. "But the garage was empty when it happened. Right?"

The old man was full of fresh astonishment. How could he know about the dead man they had hauled out of there? But the way he looked, nauseated almost, Ash had clearly anticipated the worst.

"A man was caught in there," Luke told him.

"I don't guess he got out?"

Luke shook his head.

"Dammit, Luke. I *told* you not to come up here. I told you things weren't like they used to be. This place is a powder keg with a maniac diddling with the fuse. That could just as well have been you. Cars have been blown up, too, Molotov cocktails flying out of nowhere, and now this." His voice trailed off and he turned toward the window. "Saturday. Tom Harrow spends every Saturday in that old garage he rents from Maude. Rain or shine, if he has a day off, he's in there working on that fool car of his. It was Tom, wasn't it?"

He was holding on to the arms of his wheelchair with knuckle-whitening force. The flesh of his face, runneled by time and pain, was hardened and flushed as Luke leaned to put a hand on his shoulder. Thin blades of bone under worn cotton. What about your safety? Luke wanted to shout. If it's dangerous for a young man with two legs, how about you? Instead, he shook his head. "I didn't hear the man's name," he told him. "But somebody said something that sounded like 'Nan's boy.' That's all I heard."

When Ash put out his empty hand, Luke set his drink in it. He drained the glass and set it down hard between the books on his library table. Then he lifted the glass, delicately wiped off the bottom of it, and put it down again. "Tom," he said out loud to himself.

17

His voice roughened with anger. "But he wasn't any man. Only a boy. Seventeen just past. A young, talented boy . . . an artist really, if you want the truth."

"Ash," Luke began. "I'm really sorry."

Ash shook his head and cleared his throat. "I'll get a handle on it. It just hits home." As he spoke, he turned and reached for the phone. "I've got to get hold of that boy's mother somehow."

His voice turned cross again. "Take your stuff on over to the cabin. It's readied for you. When supper's on the table, I'll ring the bell." Luke hesitated. It was hell to have to let the old man wait on him like that, but Ash had always known how to handle him. He frowned at Luke fiercely, the way he used to. "If you know what's good for you, you'll come flying in here at the first clang of that bell!"

As Luke stepped onto the porch the dog came off his rug like a shot, a dripping tongue aimed for his face. Luke was pushing him away when he heard Ash shout after him. "And don't spoil *that* dog like you did the last one!"

Chapter 2

Luke had reconstructed that cabin in his mind so many times that he hesitated before opening the door. Ash had elevated him to manhood the summer he turned sixteen by letting him move his stuff out of the spare bedroom and into that cabin. Any idiot can mouth clichés about trust. Ash put cash money on the line. You can always rent a cabin like that up in the mountains, at least for a month or two in summer. That was how Ash got hung with an extra kid in the first place. Luke's mother had rented the place, lived there a couple of years, and then died . . . leaving a four-year-old boy Ash either had to keep and raise or send down the mountain to be "fostered out," as he put it. If that place was not what he remembered, Luke was going to find it tough to deal with.

Linden had been about eight when Luke's mother died. He had always envied Linden because she had been old enough to remember his mother. He long ago quit kidding himself that he recognized the woman in the snapshots Ash gave him. His mother was more shadowy to him than the fused black-and-white lines of those photos, not visible at all, but remembered through a wordless voice, rhythmical and melodious.

Luke let out his breath in a slow whistle of relief when he stood in the open door.

The cabin was spare, with the same wood-burning stove dominating the principal room. The stove was identified as "Ashley" by a line of handsome Roman letters just above its round belly. Graceful metal legs supported it on a square slate base. Just beyond that, the room suffered an identity crisis and became a kitchen whose window, above the sink, stared bleakly into the darkness. The bedroom and bath were minuscule but adequate. Curved ornamental legs again. Luke chuckled, looking at the legs of that tub, remembering Ash waxing philosophical about them when Luke was complaining about scrubbing under there on his stomach. "Funny thing about fashion," Ash said, "the legs of bathtubs disappeared under porcelain about the time women began to show theirs off. You suppose that'll ever switch again?"

The wooden floors were blanched from the diligence of scrub brushes. Ash had said it was "readied."

With the windows open, the sounds of the forest filtered in. Crazy. Twenty-four hours earlier Luke had watched Linden Porter turn heads in a French restaurant and then sit across from him, delicately holding a crystal wineglass and talking scathingly about this place for over an hour. How could anyone hate what filtered in through those windows, wind brushing the night with restless branches, the hollow colloquy of owls?

He had written to Linden Porter as soon as he heard about Ash's accident. He had only a box number in San Francisco that Ash had sent him when she first moved away. Linden's reply came only a few days before his travel arrangements were concrete. Her note, which bore no return address, did give her phone number along with a request that he call on arrival and plan to have dinner with her that Friday night before coming up to the mountain.

The restaurant was a few blocks north and east of Union Square. It was small, maybe ten tables, and chef-run, with a staff of wiry young men bearing a strong family resemblance. The room was appealing in spite of being a little dark for his taste, the tables lit only by candles flanking bud vases of little white daisies that smelled like chrysanthemums. He got there early with a visitor's insecurity about gauging time and distance in a city turned strange to him by time.

The moment Linden came through the door he had a thrust of old childish envy. As always, Linden had it together. She was still slender, but had lost the look of fragility he remembered. She walked with the leggy confidence of a woman accustomed to turning heads. Instead of aging, she had acquired polish. Her straight black hair swayed loose to the shoulders of a rose-colored silk suit the exact shade of her lipstick. Luke had an insane urge to focus entirely on her ankles; as a boy he remembered fantasizing that he could circle one of them with a forefinger and thumb.

"Luke," she said, the inflection rising. The cheek she offered smelled expensive. The waiter got to her chair before he did. With the candle guttering from the flirt of her napkin into her lap, Luke wondered if he could possibly break through her crust of childhood resentment and make a friend of her. He had always hoped such a day would come, but Ash's condition made their cooperation vital. Between them, he and Linden ought to be able to work out a solution that would make Ash safe as well as happy.

When Luke was little, Linden's way with him had been confusing. She was quietly civil when Ash was around, only to turn bitter and caustic when they were alone. Later her resentment made sense to him. It must have been traumatic for an only kid that young to yield space in her father's life and household. It had to make it harder that he was nobody special but just a kid who got dropped there by the double accidents of geography and death.

Even though Linden couldn't have been much more than a secretary to Burt Roberts back on the mountain, she had been a class act. She was still a class act, not only knowing how to dress but clearly having money enough to afford the best. When he had called, the voice of the recording machine had given him a business name, "Porter Properties." Whatever that meant, it was keeping Linden in good threads.

There wasn't any law that you have to be able to see the pupils in the blackness of human eyes, but the total darkness of Linden's eyes disconcerted him. Why had he remembered those same eyes sparkling with sudden lights? "I was really astonished to hear from you, Luke." Her voice was unchanged from the old days. "I can't believe you really intend to go back to that mountain . . . even to visit."

He shrugged. "If there wasn't anything else, I grew up there."

"But you left," she reminded him.

"It was time." He shouldn't have to explain to her why he left. Not only was he more indebted to Ash than any man should be to another, but he was fresh from the experience of high school. She must have gone through some of that agony herself. Brains, looks, athletic ability . . . nothing gave you entry when you went down off the mountain into high school. You were a "hill kid," created to be despised. Four years of that either drove you back into the hills or as far away as you could travel. "But there is something else, Linden. I realize I haven't seen Ash yet, but no matter how strong he is, he can't be safe up there on that mountain alone. There's only you and me. I was hoping—"

"You and me and Ash," she interrupted. "Maybe you've forgotten that Ash Porter is a law unto himself.

He intends to run his own show, and I, for one, want no part of it."

Her cavalier dismissal of Luke's own consuming concern left him speechless as she went on. "Aside from seeing my father, I can't imagine what a trip back to that mountain can possibly offer a world traveler like you."

Luke looked at her. She wasn't going to get off that easy. He had come to talk to her about Ash, and he intended to talk about it whether she wanted to listen or not. In the meantime, this world traveler opening was borderline insulting. World traveler, indeed. Join the army and enjoy Europe in the last third of the twentieth century; the Red Brigade, hostage crises, oil embargoes, car bombs on American bases, and screaming demonstrations about nuclear armament, not even to mention the ubiquitous paranoia that had grown out of random terrorist attacks. "I learned things up there that have been priceless to me," he told her.

"I can't imagine how *that* could be."

Even if she had phrased that as a question he would have sidestepped answering it. Thanks to Ash's raising, he had come off the mountain green and hungry but liking himself. Only later had he learned there was nothing like the combination of dogged self-reliance with a healthy ego to help you survive in a world where both your passport and your uniform could invite disaster. But it was strange that Linden didn't phrase anything in a question. Not strange, but ridiculous. Questions and answers knit the bridge of passed time. How could two people possibly communicate for an entire evening by trading statements? And how could he possibly get through this evening without telling her exactly how he felt about her callous disregard for Ash's welfare?

But if this was her game, two could play. "I have to admit I don't know what business you're into."

She shrugged. "Investment management. Not the most exciting thing in the world." At his glance, she went on. "Stocks, bonds, the commodities market . . . you name it, I'll quote the current expectations. But it is pretty dull, all those numbers and most of them born of informed guessing."

"But you do have your own company," he said. "That must be satisfying." At her quizzical glance, he explained. "Maybe I just figured you were the Porter of Porter Properties."

She nodded. "Of course, the telephone. It is my own company, very small."

"And you are into investments. Hey." He smiled at her. "Would you believe I just bought my first lottery ticket since I got Stateside? If I win, I'll put it all in your hands and clip coupons."

Maybe she only smiled bewitchingly when she said no. "Sorry, Luke. You'll get lots of other offers. Mine is a closed corporation. All *very* dull."

A second invitation to drop it. She didn't want to talk about some sensible plan for her father. He didn't want to talk about terrorism and she didn't want to discuss investment opportunities. "Good God, Linden," he wanted to shout at her. "We grew up together. You're the closest to a sibling I ever had. You were the only woman I really knew as a child. Don't treat me like a stranger! And don't pretend that your responsibility to Ash can be swept away in a few glib phrases."

Then it struck him that whatever had driven that wedge between her and her father had not only severed her allegiance to Ash permanently but had walled him out, too. Not fair.

Then he would have to deal with Ash's situation on his own. But that still left the problem of the evening. They hadn't even ordered drinks, and already he was dredging for the next topic. Did they have mutual friends up in the mountains? His mind went blank. Then it happened. A screech of brakes, the cacophony of metal on metal, and shocked voices shouting. A siren wailed up the street outside, eliciting a furious explosion of car horns. Waiters strained discreetly over the half-drapes at the windows and a couple from another table stood, napkins in hand, to stare into the street. Linden looked over with a mild liveliness in her expression.

"That reminds me. Madrone has even made it into the city papers this summer. Fire on the mountain and all that."

Her flippant tone was grating in view of Ash's situation. "Your father takes it very seriously."

"Ash doesn't have enough to distract him, since he's tied to that wheelchair. And all his birds have flown."

Luke stared at her, puzzled. Ash was the only man he ever heard of who had kept a lifetime bird record. Even as a kid it had blown Luke away to realize that from the time Ash Porter was eight years old, he had kept a journal of every new bird he saw and recorded their species, the season he had sighted them, and where. Linden couldn't mean what it sounded like she did.

She laughed softly. "God, you're literal. I meant he hasn't any human beings under his control. I'm gone, you're gone. He rented the cabin to a woman named Nan Harrow for a couple of years, but now she and her boys, Will and Tom, are gone, too. He has nothing to think about except what he reads in that miserable rag of a paper."

She met his gaze without smiling before turning to the waiter at her side. "I'll have Tanqueray on the rocks with a twist. What will it be for you, Luke?" By the time he placed his order, she was deep in the study of the menu. She spoke quietly, her voice firm. "This is my treat, you know. My city, my treat."

"That's ridiculous," he protested.

25

Her eyebrows lifted as she looked up. "I invited *you*." Cool class.

Back to the menu again. Then it struck him. She didn't ask questions because she didn't want to give answers of her own. What had managed to toughen Linden Porter without marking that beguiling surface? Or had his loneliness as a child made him imagine the wonderful humor he remembered in her, the magnetic warmth?

She shrugged. Slender, almost bony shoulders moved the light along the drape of the rose silk. Then she took a second run at trying to talk him out of visiting Ash. "Forgive my candor, Luke, but if you can get out of this trip to the mountains, you should do it. Spend your time here in the city. San Francisco will look different and better than it did when you were twenty and broke. All you are going to find on that mountain is a time warp . . . same people, same lifestyle, same old simmering feuds. Dull."

She caught his resentment. "Okay," she said lightly. "You liked it as a kid better than I did. But I do hate to see a grown man clinging to romantic notions. And you aren't going to like the changes you find. Since you left the mountains for good reasons, you shouldn't go back unless your reasons are equally compelling."

What better reason could a man have? If Linden didn't understand how concerned he was about her dad, how deeply he loved him, and how much he was in debt to him, he couldn't get it across in the length of an evening. Anyway, he was suddenly woefully tired. The jet lag built into his flight from the East Coast had given his Scotch a quantum kick. All that sounded good to him was to sleep against the next day's long drive up into the mountains.

Maybe he could jerk himself awake by making a game of the evening, thinking of it as a contest. If he trapped Linden into asking him a question, she owed him ten million dollars. If he didn't he owed it to her.

The siren wailing outside as the ambulance started away reminded him of the fear between the lines of Ash's letter. "Tell me what *has* changed on the mountain," he suggested.

Ploys born of desperation sometimes work. She talked through the hearts of romaine piqued with a subtle vinaigrette and the pasta with scallops and morels that followed. The wine she selected arrived, was tasted, and was served, a pale glittering wine in a thin-necked green bottle.

"You know about Ash's accident," she said without meeting his eyes. She didn't pause, but he broke in anyway.

"Only that he was sideswiped by one of Larson and Frane's trucks and has been left in a wheelchair. What happened?"

She gave him the full force of these dead-black eyes. "It's a typical mountain story, I'm afraid. A loaded truck was on the straightaway between Ash's ranch and Madrone. Some idiot fired a wild shot in the woods that smashed the truck's windshield. The driver ducked. By the time he recovered himself he had sideswiped Ash and the truck had jackknifed. He was lucky to crawl out alive himself. That's a lot of weight to have flying out of control at that speed."

"Did the driver see who fired the shot? They must have had a hearing."

"They had hearings all right. Ash's hospitalization didn't come cheap to the insurer. The driver, a man named Madison Ford, was only quoted, that was all. He ended up at Maude's after the police left the accident scene. He was raving, swearing he'd get the bastard who fired that shot. Instead, he took off."

Luke stared at her. "What does that mean?"

"He took off, left the mountain before even testifying

at the hearing. They looked for him but never caught up with him."

"Why would a guy take off like that? That doesn't make sense."

"Of course it does, Luke. You have to remember that Ash was in pieces when the ambulance got there. Nobody would have given you a nickel for his chances. Ford was just an itinerant driver with no roots on the mountain. I can understand his turning chicken and running. Staying wasn't going to put Ash back together."

There was more Luke wanted to ask, but she hummed on without hesitating long enough for him to break in. "I do agree with you. Ash is a fool to stay up there in the shape he's in. He's completely vulnerable, and there's too much to do on that place even if he could find responsible help. But he's bullheaded, Luke. It's a wonder he didn't give up before the accident. This was only the last of a series of hard knocks. It started with two years of severe drought that brought a killer infestation of bark beetles. The Douglas firs around the house all had to be taken out. I guess since the accident the loss of those trees can be looked at as good or bad. The place has got to look like hell without those trees, but if Ash is going to be stubborn enough to stay there, he can at least see everything that happens on the mountain with those fancy binoculars you sent him."

"It's got to look like hell," she had said. Did that mean she hadn't even been back to see her father since his accident?

It was clearly Luke's turn to ante up something to keep the conversational pot boiling. She hadn't mentioned marijuana, the one thing everyone thought of when they heard where he was from. "How about the great cash crop I remember from the Seventies? That mountain has a worldwide reputation for producing truckloads of the best dope money can buy."

She laughed. "That used to be true, but the word got around to the federals, too. Plantings are always being burned off or chemically destroyed. They even raided one big drug factory up there, not marijuana but heavy stuff . . . recreational chemistry complete with copper vats." She tightened her shoulders and smiled. "There's a great tug-of-war going on here in the city. Some genius realized you could grow magnificent marijuana hydroponically under artificial lights. Point, counterpoint. Somebody looked at those astronomical electric bills and figured out what was going on."

"Nipped it in the bud?" he asked, amused in spite of himself.

She shook her head. "There's always a way to take an end run around the law. The city growers just install saunas or whirlpools. This gives them a double bargain, a perfect excuse for inflated power use plus capital improvements on the property."

They had worn that out. "Tell me about this arson business."

She stirred in her seat. "Stupid mountain fever of some kind. The paper keeps mentioning old feuds, but I am guessing it's some kook with a grudge to settle. Work is scarce and cash is hard to come by. The devil's workshop and all that."

Luke frowned thoughtfully. "If the drought killed a lot of trees there has to be some lumbering activity." Her glance at him was startled. Had she forgotten he had been a boy tailing a lumberman through those woods? Dead trees had to be cut down and taken out of those forests. If not, the bark beetles spread to healthy trees, or the trees caught fire in storms, or fell and damaged healthy trees. "Work is work even if it's only trees taken down for salvage."

She tightened her lips. "Salvage wood pays next to

nothing . . . a few cents a board foot when a foot of live lumber comes in close to a hundred dollars."

"I'm amazed that lumber prices have held," he told her. "Overseas we keep reading that homebuilding and general construction haven't pulled out since the recession."

She smiled at him. "You sound as if you were the one in commodities. Lumbering is down, but not as much as you'd think. The big companies gamble on futures. Those woods are full of decks of prime lumber sitting under sprinklers, waiting for the market to recover." She straightened in her chair, a signal for closure. "I hope you don't mind making this an early evening, but tomorrow is a killer day."

She cocked her head a little and leaned across the table, her perfume overwhelming the pungent scent of the daisies. "Think seriously about canceling that trek up to the Madrone. You could knock your rustic romantic illusions into a basket."

Outside, a uniformed man with a push broom was sweeping broken glass back against the curb. Linden looked at Luke doubtfully as the cab she had signaled pulled up. "Do you realize that nobody up there *ever* forgets anything? And your precious Ash is probably the worst of them."

He stared at her. Good God, that was a question. Did he owe her ten million dollars? Luke waved at her through the cab window and turned away. Rhetorical questions didn't count. Anyway, she'd only squander the ten million on fancy clothes and expensive perfume.

Ash's bell clanged from the cabin across the clearing. In a way Linden had been right. This place *did* feel like a time warp. Luke had a flash freaky memory of Ash solemnly examining his hands and face before letting him sit down to dinner.

An oval roaster held a steaming pot roast surrounded

by brown quartered potatoes and whole onions in thick gravy. Bread, butter, with an open jar of beet horseradish rounding out the fare. How did Ash manage all this—groceries in, garbage out, cooking a meal—just as he had in the old days? Never mind that he was skating on borrowed time; he was cutting a pretty fancy figure. This wasn't going to make it any easier for Luke to broach the subject of his leaving this place.

Ash was surprisingly voluble, given how depressed he had been earlier. "Everything okay over at the cabin?"

"Wonderful," Luke told him. "I heard owls talking."

Ash nodded. "I saw one earlier this week, just at dusk, hunting." He looked up brightly. "Did I write you that I sighted a great horned owl a couple of summers ago? Looked close enough to touch, thanks to your glasses. They must have cost a bundle, but it wasn't wasted. Wait'll I show you the project those binoculars of yours started me on. You aren't going to believe your own eyes."

Luke grinned to himself. That remark was pure Ash Porter for "Thanks."

"That was your first great horned owl, then?"

He nodded. "Unbelievable, those birds. They stand two feet tall with a five-foot wingspan. Farther up north they call them the 'tigers of the woods.' When one passes close you hear the whisper of death."

"Whisper of death," he repeated, echoing his own words. He pushed back his plate. "Death. After I talked to Nan Harrow, the sheriff called. The doctor was still examining Tom, but he was guessing Tom's car fell on him. crushing him. He's trying to figure out what came first, the jack slipping or the explosion and fire. The gas tank blowing up could have rocked that car off the jack. No matter how the coroner's inquest turns out, Sheriff Dodge has scheduled a hearing on Monday. He wants you to come."

"He half warned me of that. It's silly to call me in. I walked in out of the woods when the fire was already going."

"Everybody who was anywhere close will be there. If I know that courthouse down there, a lot of people who weren't within ten miles of the place will be there, too. As deputy sheriff, Dodge is deputy coroner, too. It's his job to piece some sense out of this."

"Surely the inquest will settle the cause of death."

"There's more to it than cause. A man can only die about four ways. That inquest isn't likely to come up with suicide or natural causes."

"So they only have accident or foul play?" Luke asked.

"And the means is confusing," Ash added. "With a car explosion like that, it's hard to fix whether there really was arson. That gas would be thrown around everywhere."

"But they are talking arson?"

"A couple of people reported seeing a man running right after the explosion. Sometimes they put together a strike team to investigate a multiple crime like that . . . possible arson, possible murder, and robbery to boot."

"Robbery?"

Ash nodded. "Eddie also told me he went up to check out Tom's cabin and found it had been ransacked, even the floorboards prized up."

"But you told me this Tom was just a kid. Didn't he still live with his mother?"

The question made Ash uncomfortable. He waved Luke back into his chair as he began to clear the table. "Tomorrow you can help. Tonight you're company." He shook his head. "Nan Harrow and her boys moved into that cabin where you are when they first came up on the mountain. . . . That must have been four years ago, about the time Linden took off. Nan's boy Will is a rock, but Tom went out of control this summer. God only knows what got into him. He was talented, too, but he took a crazy streak and finally just up and walked out on her."

"But how can a kid like that live?"

His voice turned distant. "Oh, different ways. He worked for me around here a little and did a lot of photography for me until I got hurt, and he's always gone sniping."

Luke had forgotten that word. For a minute his head went "sniping . . . sniper," and he pictured a rifle barrel spitting fire from a half-open window. Then he remembered sniping in the mountains was different. Boys and sometimes men panned gold along the watershed all summer, sleeping out and living on fresh trout. Luke remembered high school friends who had come out in the fall with as much money as they could have made sweating in the peach groves in the valley.

Ash handed Luke a tea towel and ordered him to help dry. One after-dinner Scotch and that high, clean air laid Luke out before nine.

Luke had one good long day with Ash before the scheduled hearing and the arsonist hit another time. When Luke got over to his place that next morning, Ash had bacon staying warm on a platter in the oven and the grease waiting for Luke's egg order.

"I don't need to spoil that dog of yours," Luke told him. "He's already rotten. I only got up this early to keep him from scratching your door down."

Ash laughed. "I sent him. I don't make biscuits to turn to rocks for slugabeds."

"You're after something," Luke said wisely. "You never made breakfast biscuits in your life without an ulterior motive."

Ash grinned. "If you can get me and my wheel into that car of yours, I'd like to take a ride. Will drives

33

me here and there when he's been around, but he's been away most of the past two weeks. I've got an acute case of cabin fever."

Did he dare take that remark as an opener? Ash didn't give him time. Instead, he looked up and smiled. "That Will Harrow is one fine boy, if you can call a man of twenty a boy. I got real attached to Nan Harrow and those kids when they were living here. Thank God Will took interest in the bees, or they would have had a tough season. While I was off in the hospital Nan and Will took care of this place, then, when I was sent home, they wore themselves out fixing up things here so I could manage."

"Had Tom already moved away from home then?"

"No, but he was on the way out. He came to see me in the hospital just once, to bring me some pictures. He wasn't really himself that day, and by the time I got home, he and Nan were at loggerheads. He had some kind of work that produced enough money to go to his head. He wouldn't even tell Nan who he was working for or what he was doing, but he got cocky and quick-tempered, not like himself at all. Naturally she was worried to death." He shrugged. "Such a talented kid. Too bad, just too bad."

Luke pushed his plate back, seeing that smoking corpse being dragged out of the inferno of that garage.

Ash's mind was still on Will. "Having Will around was almost like having you back home the way he helped me out, kept me in firewood, and tended the bees."

"Just for the record, Ash, I think you need somebody up here all the time, maybe living in that cabin . . ." Ash didn't let him finish. His face paled and he leaned toward Luke angrily.

"Don't you start that. Every busybody on this mountain has taken on my business since that accident, and I'm stuffed to the gills with it."

He fell silent and started to clear the table.

Luke watched him whip the tray into the kitchen and begin cleaning up. What kind of an argument could he put up when Ash could manage like this?

When the guys kidded Luke about staying single, he always told them he was looking for a girl who could cook and keep a kitchen as well as Ash Porter. And bring down Douglas firs, of course. Would they believe a wheelchair? That sink and stove shone when he loaded Ash and his chair into the car and set out with him, binoculars over Ash's thin shoulder.

It was easy enough to see what Ash wanted to look at. They set off toward the north, where a thin wavering of smoke rose above the tops of the trees. "I noticed that smoke this morning and hoped it was a slash pile," Luke told him.

Ash nodded. "It was a big one, too. It was already good-sized when I got hurt last spring. It's been smoking there a week or two now. Another good rain should damp it out."

The roads Ash pointed out led around and through the timber stands he could see from his naked hill. Most of them were on federal land. Luke recognized one of the streams they passed. He had panned out a nugget the size of a pea there the year he was ten. He'd never felt that rich again.

Ash told him to stop near the smoking slash pile. "A colony of owls used to live right in here," he said wistfully. No homes were left for owls anymore. A wide area had been cleared to make room for the slash pile. Because a pine needle was damned near a volatile oil, debris from the lumbering sites was piled up in open clearings like this one all through the dry season. Cats pushed huge limbs and scrub trees along with a fair amount of dirt to form giant pyres forty or fifty feet across and twice a man's height. Potential bonfires like that made people edgy. The last thing anybody wanted was a slash pile being fired by accident when the woods were dry. From the way this pile was smoldering down, he knew Ash was right about when it was fired.

More than once Ash told him to stop while he studied the trees with those glasses of his. Most of the stands he looked at were clean and healthy, but in some of them red plastic flags fluttered on the trunks, marking them to be cut for salvage. But Linden was right. The lumbering was going on unchanged from what Luke remembered. In some clearings, giant trees had been cut in lengths, ready for the choke setters to set with cables for the tractors to haul away. He tried to avoid glancing at the man in the seat beside him. It had to be hell for Ash to be trapped in a rolling chair after spending his life in those woods.

They had lunch in a tavern in Bardenville that had yuppie aspirations and a salsa cruda that burned straight through the top of Luke's head. Passing Burt Roberts's place at sunset, Ash pointed at the sign with the horse on it. "Burt Roberts's young wife is a noted horse-woman. Medals and awards from all over." Luke was surprised at the tinge of pride in Ash's voice. But Ash favored young people, always had, and if that girl was anything like as young as she looked, he would have some special indulgence for her.

"She's as pleasant and friendly as she is pretty, too," Ash went on. "Burt's gone a lot, and she comes riding up here on one of those fancy horses. She claims to come for honey, but she always stays and visits like she was lonesome. She was raised down in San Francisco, the only child of a San Francisco banker who went into vineyards early. There's big money behind her. But she's got an expensive hobby, too. She breeds Arabians. I can't figure what she saw in Roberts, but he isn't the first old head to be turned by a saucy ass."

"He can be pretty flashy on his own," Luke pointed

out. "I remember pictures from a safari he went on, Great White Hunter business. And he always brings in his limit during deer season."

"Sure," Ash snorted. "It's real flashy when a man kills for sport what his neighbor needs for food."

"Well, he isn't exactly ancient," Luke said.

Ash glared at him. "He's seven years older than Linden, and she's no kid anymore."

The fresh air had been good for Ash. He sat contentedly staring into the woods with his binoculars while Luke fed the dog and made sandwiches from the leftover pot roast and some bread and butter pickles he found in the fridge. By the time they finished supper and Luke cleaned up the mess, Ash's eyes were at half-mast.

Luke started out of the door with a drink to take back to his cabin. Bandit wagged him out of it. He sat by the dog on Ash's front steps, wondering how he was ever going to find the guts to talk to Ash again about moving off this hill. When he couldn't answer that question, he stared at the rental cabin. Maybe he could locate a couple who would take the place rent-free in barter for what maintenance and work Ash needed done.

The one thing he couldn't do was leave again with Ash this vulnerable.

Chapter 3

Ancient palm trees jutted from the carefully barbered lawns around the county courthouse in Featherton. The building was constructed of rough gray stone, striated with the high-water marks of a century of floods.

The results of the coroner's inquest were announced. Tom Harrow had died of a sharp blow to the head by a blunt instrument, presumed from the lesion to have been a monkey wrench. The absence of smoke in his lungs indicated that he was dead, rather than unconscious, when the car fell off the jack and the fire started. The finding was suspicion of murder. The county attorney, dapper in gray, conducted the questioning with brisk disinterest.

But the locals from Madrone were all there. Eddie Dodge, in a fresh shirt with his belly tucked inside, drew a line through Luke's name on a yellow legal pad and motioned him to a seat. The most formal thing about the ceremony was that each witness went forward to be sworn in before telling his story. The statements ranged from brief to meandering. Faces acquired names, some of which Luke vaguely remembered.

Everyone knew Tom Harrow. Two women visiting over coffee had seen him go into the garage about a half hour before the explosion. Those who hadn't seen him presumed he was there.

"But you didn't see him go in there?" the attorney asked.

"Listen," the second woman protested. "When you hear the thump and thunder of that rock music shaking the roof wall of that garage, you know Tom is in there tinkering with that car of his."

The report of a man running off toward the woods behind Maude's Place came from Rick Boniface, a rangy young man with an open but concerned expression, who had been saddling a horse when the explosion came. The horse had reared on him, but he had caught that glimpse in the very corner of his eye. No, he had no idea whether the man was young or old, but he was moving fast. As far as that went, it could have been a woman, for all he knew. It was somebody wearing pants.

Burt Roberts was called up next. Roberts looked older in the raw midafternoon light, less rakish and daring with the smudges of smoke cleaned from his face. According to Burt Roberts, he and his wife, Amie, and Bo Sanders, a forester in his employ, were sitting over lunch in Maude's when the blast came. A rancher and his wife and two other men testified in corroboration.

They'd all been at Maude's, too, and damned near got shook out of their chairs.

Had any of them left the place at any time?

"I went to the men's room," Roberts offered. "And Amie here," he nodded at his wife, "went out to the kitchen to ask Maude something."

"She wanted to know what kind of cheese I had put on the burgers," Maude volunteered from her seat. The benches creaked as people turned to stare at her. "Monterey Jack," she said, crossing her hands on her stomach and settling back again before the judge got out his request that she hold her statement until she was called.

"Was Mrs. Roberts still in the kitchen when the blast came?"

Maude nodded. "We both damn near jumped out of our shoes right there."

"But you were back at your table by then?" he asked Roberts, who nodded.

Luke watched Burt Roberts's wife testify, remembering what Ash had said about her. She looked young enough. Luke would have guessed her at twenty-one. Ash's description, "a pretty little thing," fell way short of the mark. By any man's standard, she was beautiful. Her features were delicately defined, good high cheekbones with an angle to her jaws that gave her face the shape of a heart. Her luminous skin looked transparent, and her eyes, raised to the attorney's questions, were oddly tilted, not really slanted but set differently enough to be noticeable. She was wearing a long, full skirt with a loose gauze blouse that made her appear even more fragile than she had seemed in the brief glance he had of her the day before. When she mounted the stand she corroborated her husband's statement in a low, clear voice that was devoid of either expression or emotion.

Bo Sanders identified himself as a forester and assistant to Burt Roberts.

When Sanders's statement, delivered in a low, husky voice, supported the others, he was sent back to his seat. Sanders, along with his employer and wife, were the three best-looking as well as the three best-dressed people in the room.

Luke snapped from his daydreaming when Silas Engel rose and took the chair. He couldn't believe the old man was still around. Although Ash always insisted he was harmless, Engel had scared Luke to death a half-dozen times when Luke was a kid. Engel was

40

forever prowling in the woods, appearing suddenly like a looming wraith out of the darkness of the woods. You never knew where to expect him. Back then he had always been searching for a dog somebody had stolen from him. Now it was a cow.

Silas Engel had the dust of those ten years on him. His suspenders dropped like plumb lines from the curve of his shoulders to his trousers, hanging free of his shallow chest. When asked his whereabouts at the time of the fire, he launched into a catalogue of calumny and threat, accusing Eddie Dodge of persecuting him, challenging the honesty and motives of everyone who had made a statement. He waggled a cautionary finger at the crowd, threatening revenge for their thievery and low-down rottenness. Several times he mentioned a vengeful God and kept coming back to a cow named Boss that had been stolen away in the night. The attorney, flushed with impatience, was finally able to wedge him, still ranting, out of the chair and back to his seat so he could call the next witness.

Luke Adams.

Luke carefully recited again what he had done the day of the fire, then had to repeat it a dozen ways to answer the questions. He was fighting to concentrate on what the attorney was asking. From the moment he took the chair that faced the room, he had found himself distracted by a woman on the back row whom he knew he had never seen before. She was not the sort of person he would have forgotten.

She was a small, solid woman with wide-set eyes in an unseamed face. Her hair was a good half-dozen shades of brown in the light streaming in through a tall, narrow window. It looked long enough to hang below her shoulders if she had released it from the knotted bandanna that bound it back. Her body looked athletic and deceptively young in jeans and a faded plaid shirt. The way she held her lips straight together, folded in a little on themselves, telegraphed bitter wisdom and pain. Luke wouldn't have taken a guess at her age for his life. But neither could he look at her without it hurting. The questions droned on. "Tell me again, Luke Adams, how you happened to be passing along the road when the fire broke out."

"I was on my way to Ash Porter's place."

The attorney consulted a paper in his hand. "And you are the boy he informally adopted and raised up after your mother died up there in his rental cabin? I believe she called herself Belle Adams."

"Her name was Isabelle Adams," Luke told him. What did all this have to do with arson and murder, if murder was what they were talking about? He met the man's eyes angrily.

"And where were you coming from?"

"Munich, Germany," Luke told him. "By way of Baltimore and San Francisco."

"Saturday you just told the deputy the army."

Luke sighed. "I am on leave. Saturday I was coming in from San Francisco, where I had visited with Linden Porter, Ash Porter's daughter." The attorney stared at him a moment, then told him to step down.

Luke felt eyes watching him pass, Burt Roberts and Amie, Maude from the café, even old Silas Engel of the lost cow Boss. Only Bo Sanders didn't look up. He kept his eyes down, studying his own hands.

Before her name was even called, Luke realized that the woman on the back row had to be Nan Harrow.

She walked past him, saying more in the lines of her body than any of them had managed to express in their rambling statements. She put her feet down straight in a line, walking loose from the hip, not cocky, not even confident, just knowing where she was going and that she was strong enough to make the trip.

The attorney's mumbled condolences were humiliating. She nodded acknowledgment of them, her wide-set eyes steady on his face.

Why would anyone force so many questions on a woman who had just lost a son violently? She hadn't even been there when it happened. Yet the man went on with his tedious flow of questions, some of dubious relevancy.

Nan Harrow had not seen her son Tom that morning, nor talked to him.

She was not surprised that he was in under the car tinkering, since he generally spent his free time fooling with the car.

No, she didn't know where he was working during the week.

She knew of no enemy who bore him ill will.

Where was her son Will, Tom's brother, at the time of fire and explosion?

"Out of the state," she replied.

The attorney paused, then gathered courage. "On what business?"

"His own business, and mine."

"You will forgive me," he pressed on. "It seems remarkable that your son did not return at once to be at your side."

She looked at him levelly. "What could he do?" she asked.

He seemed inclined to answer that question, looked at her a moment, and thought better of it.

"You've been apprised that an examination of your son's cabin after the fire showed it to have been ransacked?"

At her nod, he went on. "Do you have any idea what the burglars might have been after?"

"Tom has never had a bank account that I know of."

"It would be helpful to the law to have an inventory of any valuables that might have been stolen."

"I can't help you there."

"It has been reported that he often carried expensive photographic equipment around with him, a costly camera with a collection of lenses and sometimes a folded tripod. Do you have any idea where that equipment is?"

"I haven't known where he kept anything since he moved to his own place."

The attorney didn't handle frustration well. His tone became cranky. "Well," he said. "According to Deputy Dodge's report, whoever invaded your son's cabin missed finding his cache. Deputy Dodge either had better luck or more time. Do you have any idea how your son came by over seven thousand dollars in uncirculated twenty-dollar bills?"

Luke watched Nan Harrow as she waited for the murmur in the room to abate. The flesh of her face appeared to harden, and her lips went white along that fold. Her words were enunciated with immaculate precision. "He has talked about buying a new car for a long time."

"Seven thousand dollars?" the attorney challenged her.

When she only looked at him, he sighed and signaled her to step down.

Ash's house was dark as Luke pulled into the clearing after the inquest. When Bandit came pounding out to greet him, the light went on inside. As a kid, Luke had been convinced Ash could see in the dark from the way he walked silently through the woods at night, watching for birds and knowing them by name after the light was all gone.

Ash's nap hadn't made him look any fresher. His eyes looked tired and his smile of greeting showed effort. He ordered Luke to draw them both a Scotch and tell him what had gone on.

He leaned forward, frowning, when Luke got to Nan Harrow's statement. "How did she look?" he asked. "Plumb worn out, I guess."

"I have nothing to compare it with," he told him. "She seemed very much in control."

He nodded. "Nan is good at control."

"The attorney tried to get Nan Harrow to tell him what business her son Will was off on."

He grunted. "I'd wager he didn't get far on that. Nan is not known for loose talk, either." He emptied his glass and handed it to Luke for a refill. "So Tom's place had been torn up," he said. "Anything said about a camera?"

Luke looked up in surprise. "Matter of fact, it was mentioned. When the attorney mentioned it, I figured he was trying to get Nan Harrow to tell him what might be missing from the cabin."

"What did she say?"

"She said she didn't know where he kept the camera or the lenses. Something special about that camera?"

"That equipment is worth a lot. I know. I bought it."

"Was he into photography?"

Ash stirred. "I started him in it a couple of years ago. That boy was a natural artist. He would come home from sniping or fooling around in the woods and draw me a picture of some bird he'd seen. I tell you, he was talented, like another Audubon. But he wasn't taken with drawing, so I got him onto a camera by asking him to start a project for me. I've mentioned it to you before. You'll see it and know what I mean about his being talented. But that equipment was worth more than anything else in his cabin. Or this one."

"Except the money," Luke said.

"Money," Ash repeated. "How much did you say it was?"

Luke knew darn well Ash had heard the first time,

but he was like that. If you told him something preposterous, he would let it go by and ask you another time to see if you had the guts to lie twice. "Seven thousand dollars in new twenty-dollar bills."

"I guess I need to make some phone calls," he told Luke. "I bet you'd like a little time by yourself before supper. You still like a good Spanish omelet, don't you?"

Luke grinned. "My sanity is intact. Anything around here you need to have done?"

"There'll be time for that later."

Luke had never found another Spanish omelet that came within a mile of Ash's. "How do you manage on groceries?" he asked.

"I call Ruby and charge," Ash told him. "The next person passing up this road drops them off to me. If you're thinking I can't run my life from this chair, you're wrong."

When Luke finished clearing up, Ash pulled out a drawer in the library table. "I bet you've even forgotten how to play a decent hand of cards. Let's see you deal."

They played pinochle and Ash won. Ash hated conversation during cards, but there were things Luke was curious about.

"This Bo Sanders. Is he any kin to the Sanders girl I went to school with, the one who lived up near Bardenville?"

"No chance. That family spells their name with a *u* in it. Anyway, he was sent down here from Oregon by the company just this past summer."

"I thought Roberts always picked his own men."

"That's the way he likes to do it. A man don't invariably get what he likes. Like, I want to play cards and you seem to be set on having a social chat."

Luke chuckled and looked down on his loser of a

hand. Ash kept winning until even he was embarrassed. Before Luke went off to his cabin, he promised himself he would replace the fifth of whiskey they had killed.

The dog raised Cain until Luke let him in to sleep on the daybed in the living room.

Luke groaned and tried to haul himself to his feet. He didn't know whether it was Bandit's crazy barking or the pounding at the door that woke him when there was still only half-light beyond the window. At the door, he groaned again. He was certain that Eddie Dodge wasn't his idea of how to start a day.

"What's the big idea?" Luke challenged him.

"I guess you're going to say you've been here all night."

"I am going to say that, because I was," Luke told him, standing firm in the door with Bandit losing his mind behind him. Eddie shouldered past him anyway to look around the room. Bandit slid between the two men, his legs braced and his back hair stiff as a scrub brush.

"Come on, Eddie," Luke said. "Cut the heroics. Where else did I have to go? Ash and I killed a fifth and I was sleeping it off. What did you have in mind?"

"Fire," he said, watching Bandit warily. His hand jerked a little toward his hip holster every time the dog growled. Luke caught Bandit's ruff and hauled him, whining with complaint, to the door and put him out.

"Another house was fired last night," Eddie said, relaxing. "If Rick Boniface and his family hadn't been sleeping in the woods, they'd have ended up like Tom Harrow."

Boniface. He was the young man at the inquest who had been wrestling a rearing horse and seen the running figure. "So what has that got to do with me?"

"When he heard that explosion in his place, he went

47

running. He got there in time to see a car pull away, a white car like that one you got out there."

Luke studied Eddie Dodge. Had he overestimated this man? Even though he couldn't stand the guy, he never thought of him as worse than passing stupid. "Is that how he described it, Eddie? A white car like that one out there?"

The deputy looked at Luke steadily, then stretched his neck a little to one side. "Look, Adams. We were boys together, and now we're men. We didn't care much for each other then and we don't have to be buddies now, but this is damned serious business. People are dying. You heard me say Rick hauled his wife and kids out into the woods to sleep. That's out of fear, Luke. Fear is dangerous stuff. Scared folks lose their heads, go off half-cocked and make big mistakes."

"Okay," Luke conceded. "I don't think arson and murder are funny either. But neither does it amuse me for you to come flying up here and rack me out of bed because somebody spotted a white car and that's what I have rented."

Dodge shook his head, still trying. "It's not that simple. Boniface took down that license plate number. When you get into a sheriff's uniform, you get access. The computer tracked down that plate. It was on the car rented out to you."

The dog whined and clawed at the outside of the door while Luke put that together. "Okay, Eddie. Either Boniface is lying to you or somebody took that car of mine off in the night."

"You got the keys?"

"Of course I've got the keys." He fished for his pants and handed Eddie the tagged ring out of the pocket.

"You stand here and hand me those keys and then say you didn't take that car out last night?"

"Come on, Eddie. You show me a mountain boy

48

who can't hot-wire a car and I'll change his diapers for him. I don't get all this. That garage fire wasn't the first. According to Ash, you had this firebug up here before I came. Why pick on me?"

"Honest to God, Luke, what do you expect me to do when somebody reports seeing a car pull away from a bombed house? I don't know what's going on here any more than you do. But Rick Boniface is as level a guy as you could ask for. And he took down that number. A guy whose house is burning down in the middle of the night doesn't make up license numbers. What else can I do but follow up on it? First you turn up in the woods behind that garage with Tom burning up in it, then your car gets spotted outside of Boniface's. How do I know it wasn't you Rick Boniface saw running at the fire Saturday and you wanted to get rid of a witness?"

Luke shook his head. Since he was holding the pants, he pulled them on. "What possible motive would I have, Eddie?" Luke tried to keep his voice patient. "I've been away from this mountain for ten years. All I know about what's gone on here is what Ash told me in letters and Linden caught me up on the other night. I came back to see how Ash was getting along, and I came at a bad time."

"You sure as hell did," he said. "This is the worst I've ever seen it. Sure, there have always been fires on the mountain, storm fires and an occasional lit fire when somebody was drunk or mad. Nothing like this. Because the papers have been talking feud, the sheriff is on me like a deer tick. Where is a guy supposed to look for a feud? There's always been a running feud between the little lumber guys and companies like Larson and Frane. It's like the thing that goes on between the federal drug men and the folks that grow hash. People plant, and the feds come in and raid. But that's common hassling, a sort of cat-and-mouse game.

But when folks start dying, it's past hassling and way past games. The newspaper people started the feud talk, and they won't let it drop. They can't name any names, or don't, but they run it anyway, just to make news. And to be honest, if I was party to a feud and needed somebody to come in and fight on my side, you might be one I'd send for, if we was friends."

Luke stared at him. Bandit was still scratching and clawing at the closed door. Luke didn't mind replacing a fifth of Scotch, but a paneled door was a bit much. "You're not suggesting that somebody I'm tied up with is party to this arson and murder. There's only Ash, you know."

When Dodge's hesitation hung on that one moment too long, Luke shook his head.

Number one: don't blow off at this idiot.

Number two: don't let your voice give away your disgust at his stupidity.

He spoke on the count of three. "Okay, Eddie." He kept the words coming out slowly. "You got an old man who is crippled up in a wheelchair. He doesn't have chick nor child up here on this mountain, much less an accomplice to defend him or do his dirty work. Yet you want me to believe he's running around pitching Molotov cocktails. And what about this business with Jerry Hodges? Jerry and Ash Porter have been friends since Jerry and I were kids growing up. How would *his* death fit into this feud theory of yours?"

"Hell, Luke, it's not my theory. It's just going around. And things have been bad up here these past years. We had two years of drought, and a lot of people lost good trees. Then the recession with no work for anybody and no cash crops to speak of. A man could brood about that and decide to take steps against folks he thought had injured him."

"Men in wheelchairs don't take steps."

Dodge flushed. "I'm trying not to fight with you,

Luke, and I don't mean I necessarily suspect Ash Porter. But his name has come up. He's not a man to measure out words, and people up here remember what's been said. You know where Jerry Hodges was when that truck went sky-high?"

Because Luke didn't know, he waited.

"On the road right at the end of Ash's drive, that's where. Ash claims Jerry and him had talked maybe an hour. Jerry wasn't more than a few feet down the hill before his rig blew sky-high."

Luke studied him. "Why did he park out on the road where anybody could have come along and fooled with his truck?"

"Old battery. Ash said that was Jerry's reason to leave the truck out there on the road, and Hodges's widow Evie backed him up." Dodge hesitated again. "Look, Luke, somebody is behind all this, and my job's on the line to find out who it is. Ash wasn't charged. There was just talk because he's been a bitter man since that accident last spring. He's done strange things like break off with old friends. Take Tom Harrow. He and that boy used to be thicker'n thieves before this summer just past."

"Well, I understand *that*," Luke told him. "Ash tells me the boy had turned wild on his mother. That's not the kind of behavior Ash has ever put up with. I know."

Dodge studied him a moment, then shook his head. "You could be right. But I'll stick to my guns. Tom's always been a real pest. He just got worse as he got older. He turned everybody's stomach acting the big shot this summer. Anyway, with Ash like he is, and his being the last man to see Jerry Hodges alive, there's talk. Look, Adams, I'm leaning over backwards. You know I could take you in on suspicion given Rick Boniface's word alone." He jerked his head toward the other house. "Ash can't testify you were out here in this cabin all night. All I've got is your word and what comes out of the soil samples I took off that car out there."

"Hell, Eddie, I drove Ash all over this mountain in that car Sunday. You could get enough soil samples to set up a laboratory off that thing."

"I'm obliged to have them tested," he said. "I'm going to file a report saying you claim somebody must have jumped your car and took it off. We can see what reaction that gets. In the meantime, Luke, for God's sake, lie low."

Ash had wheeled to the open door and was eating the dust from Dodge's car when Luke got over to his place. "What was that all about?" Ash asked.

"Oh, you know Eddie Dodge," Luke said, stalling. The old man was tired and hung over. He was still plainly shattered by what had happened to Nan's boy. He needed this fresh dose of news real bad. But even as Luke used that tone about Eddie, he felt guilty. Eddie might be dumb, but clearly he was trying to be fair. He really *could* have hauled Luke in.

"I know Eddie Dodge, and I also know he's the law," Ash replied. "What was he doing on my place?"

"Rick Boniface's house was fired last night." Luke went on fast, not giving Ash any time to respond. "The family's okay, but Boniface gave Eddie the license number of my car."

Ash hit his palm with his fist. "Dammit, Luke, I *told* you not to come."

What could he say? "Okay if I start breakfast?" he asked, passing the old man to go back to the kitchen.

As Luke pulled the iron skillet off its hook, he heard Ash behind him blow his breath out in a hard, angry stream. By the time Luke got the bacon all laid out to cook, Ash had wheeled into the kitchen and was setting knives and forks on the table. His tone was thoughtful. "If anyone tinkered with that car last night, Bandit would have raised hell."

He might as well get it over and take his medicine. "Bandit slept in the cabin with me."

Ash slammed the rest of the silverware down hard. "I *told* you not to spoil that dog, too."

It felt good to laugh. "Okay, Ash. Point made. I'd be mad, too, if I wasn't so damned confused."

Ash's hands stopped moving, but he didn't look up. "Eddie got any theories he'll talk about?"

Luke pulled Ash's own trick back on him, standing with his back to him, too busy to look around. "Nothing he hasn't read in the papers," Luke told him.

Chapter 4

More than the heaviness of warm air told Luke that Wednesday would be a scorcher for this mountain. At only a little after seven, a faint, delicate hum was already audible from the colonies of bees just beyond the cabin doorway. The bees, their wing shapes blurred from the rapidity of their movements, hovered, already fanning to lower the hives' interior temperature. They were thirsty, too. The surface of the wet gravel filling the old truck tire under the gutter drain was velvety with tumbling yellow masses of bees jostling each other for drink.

Bandit had kept vigil. As Luke stepped onto the porch, the dog launched himself across the clearing, clutching a ragged stick between his teeth. Luke wrestled it from him and threw it toward the abandoned barn. The wood struck the upside-down watering trough with a metal clang. Luke winced to remember the dressing-down Ash had given him for turning that old trough upright just before an autumn rain.

Ash had shouted him out of the house before he had his clothes on. "Come over here, boy, and look at what you've done." As Luke looked down in horror at the dead bees floating of the surface of the trough, Ash had gone on in a tone of mingled pain and anger. "These are our bees, and by taking them on, we take on their protection. They depend on us. A man doesn't lay traps like that for creatures who depend on him." Under the cloud of Ash's disapproval, Luke had spilled out the gathered water, which peppered the barnyard earth with curled golden corpses of drowned bees.

Ash was already dressed; the smell of coffee fresh in the room. He hadn't put on his everyday clothes.

"You're pretty fancy," Luke told him, watching the old man peer into the tilted oval mirror, his eyes half closed as he tried to focus over his cheekbones at the loose folds of a dark spotted tie.

Ash grunted, tugged the knot into line, and looked up at him. "Funeral."

Luke's gut tightened involuntarily. Tom Harrow. The boy had died on Saturday. Five days had passed. He glanced at the Seth Thomas clock above Ash's bookshelf. "Maybe I better go back and dress again."

Ash shook his head. "You've no call to go."

Luke stared at him. This was ridiculous. If nothing else, the old man needed to be driven down to the church. "I feel the call," he told him.

Luke's headshake was firm. "I weighed it this way and that. You came as a stranger to that boy and never knew him in life. There'll be enough folks pretending grief at that funeral without your adding to it."

"You don't make much of a case for that boy."

He shrugged. "The old gets points when they die. Their years smudge over how they started out, so that folks only recall the man they last knew, not the wild, whipping twig he once was. Tom couldn't have picked a worse time to die."

"Was I a wild whipping twig?" Luke asked, charmed as always by the way Ash likened trees to men and men to trees.

"Not like Tom." He scowled at Luke. "Not that you were any treat to raise, mind you, but nothing like that Tom. He hadn't been on this hill more than

55

six months before he had put a chip on half the shoulders on this mountain."

"You said they came four years ago. What was he then, about thirteen?"

Ash nodded. "But give Tom fair; he was bored. Coming out of the city, he was used to more going on. This mountain might have been a cage for the way he prowled, always underfoot, always where he didn't need to be. That was how he crossed Burt Roberts in the beginning. Tom went for gold along the streams running past the company's operation until Roberts finally threatened the kid to stay off or take the consequences."

"For safety's sake, I guess," Luke mused.

"Did I tell you I've had grosbeaks around here all summer?" Luke asked. Luke didn't remember the old man's habit of changing subjects abruptly without warning. Maybe that had come in the years he'd been away.

"Grosbeaks?"

"You know, the ones with the big, thick bills for cracking seeds," Ash explained. "They aren't rare here, but I've never seen them in such numbers. They still don't even have a suspect in Tom's murder. They told me when they called about the funeral."

Luke didn't envy Eddie Dodge his badge on this one. Everybody in that village had known that boy was in that garage that afternoon.

"So how are you going to get down the mountain if I don't take you to the funeral?" Luke asked him.

"I got along before you came back," Ash reminded him. "Just like I'm going to get along after you leave. I got friends, and one is coming by." He wheeled briskly to the kitchen. "If you stick in some more toast, I'll open fresh honey."

Luke looked after him. He had blown that one. Ash was just waiting for him to challenge his ability to take care of himself again. "There was honey left in the jar from yesterday," Luke told him.

"It's gone now. I stirred it into hot milk to get myself to sleep."

"There's a fresh bottle of whiskey up there," Luke told him.

Ash grinned, his blue eyes suddenly sparkling. "I put some of that in, too. Mead, they call it."

"Yeah, mead." The honey coiled from the spiraled wooden dipper to fan swiftly on the hot toast. "Am I kidding myself, or is this bottle late-summer honey?"

Ash failed to conceal his delight. "Either you're bluffing or you've kept your old palate. This is from blackberry blooming."

"You don't taste the like of this in a mess hall," Luke told him. "Speaking of the army, one thing about it. A man loses the knack of doing nothing."

"You asking what I want done around here?"

Luke laughed. "Something like that."

"Work's as common as thieves. Pick what you fancy. There's always room in the woodbox, and brush to trim back."

"When were the bees last checked?"

Ash sighed. "Will meant to get to it, but he took off too fast on this last trip of his. We could take a couple of supers off the old hives anytime."

Another word he hadn't heard used that way since he left the mountain. The hives in spring sat low, boasting only the brood chamber and a single box above for honey storage. As the bees harvested the summer blooming, additional boxes, or supers, were added until each hive became a square wooden tower stacked up from its base.

Bandit had thundered off the porch to threaten a blue sedan inching down the drive toward the house. Ash shoved himself back from the table. "Evie's early. You might fire up the pot again."

"Evie who?" Luke asked as he scraped to his feet.

"Hodges," Ash called over his shoulder. "Make like you remember her, even if you don't."

Luke didn't remember Jerry Hodges's wife Evelyn. Jerry hadn't even married yet when Luke left the mountain. But she was a nice-looking girl with an apple forehead that gleamed from the same warmth that had set the bees to early fanning. Her eyes looked deeply set, but that could be an optical illusion. He recognized the faint discoloration around her dark eyes as being the penalty of tears. She caught his hand briefly, then sank into a chair.

"You're early," Ash said. "There's time for coffee."

She nodded. "I'd love it. I didn't have the heart this morning myself."

"You sure you want to go through with this?" Ash asked. Luke, feeling intrusive, deliberately clattered getting a fresh cup down for her. Her face was square with deep dimples that were painfully frivolous under the expression in her eyes. Looking at her brought Jerry Hodges, vital, deep-chested, and smiling, full into Luke's mind. He didn't hear her answer, but the dimples tightened up at him in a half smile as he handed her the coffee.

"This is a mighty poor homecoming for you, Luke," she said. "How long can you stay here with Ash?"

No one had asked before. "I have a full month," he told her. "That's a long time. I figured on knowing when my welcome was wearing out."

Ash grunted. "That'll be when the work's caught up. Any word of Will Harrow, Evie?"

She shook her head. "There's word he isn't going to make it to the funeral."

"Good Lord," Ash exploded. "What's into that boy? Doesn't he know Nan needs him?"

"Nan's talked to him. If she wanted him here, you know he'd come." Her voice turned harsh. "Anyway, you know better than that, Ash. Funerals are for show, just ostrich dances folks have to go through with. Nothing helps. Nothing."

When Ash leaned to touch her free hand, she caught at it desperately. "Maybe it will help when they get who's doing this."

"Foul play, person or persons unknown?" she asked, her voice tight with bitterness. "It's a good thing I'm not a betting woman. I might put our homestead up against Tom's murderer or Jerry's ever being brought to account."

The woodbox was first. Stripped to the waist, Luke hefted a log from the pile beside the chopping stump. Something swifter than his eye rustled and stirred a path under the matted leaves. Above him a scrub jay screamed, rocking with the force of his protest. Home.

His old chopping rhythm was hard to find, but when the first log split, filling the air with the rich scent of pitch, Luke grinned to himself and settled to the job. He had worked up a sweat by the time he got the woodbox filled. He stood and stretched to stand eye-level with an upside-down lizard poised on minute claws, the fold of skin across its papery throat throbbing frantically. With a flick of its tongue, it spiraled out of view.

Since the brush didn't need cutting back, Luke considered the bees. The colonies had been moved closer to the cabin. Of course, that was to take advantage of what shade was left. Hot bees swarm. Did he dare approach them after all this time?

Ash's equipment was stored, as always, in the pitch-roofed shed that served as a back porch. Luke had lit the smoker before he remembered that the smell of human sweat was almost as exciting to the bees as their own venom. He put the smoker out, showered, and heated the last of the coffee to read up on what he was tackling. Ten years was a long time.

Ash's bible on bees was by Root. First copyright, 1877. A dusty plastic kitchen bag lay beside it. Luke opened the bag and examined the syringe and medicine bottle thoughtfully. What in hell was this? The label on the bottle had curled away. Straightened, it identified a drugstore in Bardenville and the physician's name, Meyers.

Ash and Evelyn Hodges had been gone two hours. Luke replaced the book on the shelf and found Dr. Meyers's name in the directory. "He's just in from Tom Harrow's funeral," the woman told him. "Hold a minute."

So what was he going to say?

"This is Ash Porter's son," he began. "I'm home on leave."

"Of course." The voice was hearty. "Just saw Ash a few minutes ago. Got a problem?"

"I'm not sure," Luke admitted. "He's not much for talking about his health, but I ran across a syringe and a bottle of something here and wondered what that was about."

"On that table of his, I hope," the doctor interrupted.

"Not exactly," Luke told him. "Up on a bookshelf."

"That old fool. Yell at him, I have. He's so sensitized to bee stings that I'm not sure anything could save him if he tangled with those pets of his. That prescription *might* give him enough borrowed time to phone for help."

"That bad?"

"You bet your life. Bee venom isn't anything to fool around with if you're inoculated. The smart thing would be to get those colonies off that land. Actually, the really smart thing would be for him to move off that hill into town, where he would have people around to give him a hand when he needed it."

"That's what I came home to do," Luke admitted. "So far, I might as well have saved the fare."

"My sympathy. I've tried to tell Ash things he didn't

want to hear. I know what you're facing. But you could do him the favor of bolting the syringe and medicine to that chair of his."

Instead, Luke blew the dust off the plastic bag and set it on Ash's table. Lifting the binoculars, he trained them beyond the window to the clearing beyond. A single bee, caught in his focus, exploded into a giant with bubbled eyes and richly laden legs. The farther view was one of regal dimension. The smoke was still rising from the burning stash pile, but it fanned out just above the treetops, pressed down by the hot, wet air. No wonder Ash had wanted to drive the backroads. The view from his window commanded a world: the glint of a stream in the sun, the truncated curl of a road and the forest, brightened here and there by the fluttering plastic ribbons of the foresters.

When Bandit set up his alarm, Luke laid the binoculars down. From the porch he watched Evelyn Hodges's nervous shepherding of her blue sedan down the drive.

Evie refused Ash's invitation to come in for coffee or a drink. "I make it a practice to do two impossible things every day," she told him. "It's time to get the second one over with."

Ash nodded and thanked her again. He motioned Luke to wait until she had backed the car around and disappeared behind the curve in the drive.

"You people are all cryptic," Luke told him, following the awkward passage of Ash's chair over rough ground.

"If cryptic means we don't mouth things the other guy already knows, I guess we are."

"I guess the second hard thing is going back to that house without Jerry," Luke said. "But what was the first?"

Ash's tone was impatient. "How about leaving a

house to face curiosity and pity where you used to see envy?"

"Envy?" Luke asked.

"Good God, Luke, Jerry Hodges was a man, a real man, and those two had a marriage, a real marriage. You gonna tell me that's not rare where you been?"

The question must have been rhetorical, because Ash didn't wait for an answer. Or maybe mountain people didn't wait for answers they already knew either. Ash was through the house and into the kitchen, peering into the refrigerator and then banging the cupboard doors. "You need to make a run to the store," he told Luke. "Nan Harrow's coming to have supper with us."

"How come?"

"I asked her."

"Now, come on, Ash. I may have forgotten a lot, but I remember funerals. People coming piling into the house carrying every kind of cake known to woman, and hams, and keeping salads . . . "

"Nan made it plain she wasn't going back home. There was food at the church, but she wouldn't carry any away."

"This isn't making any sense to me. Why isn't she going back home?"

"She'll go home, all right. I figure she was just trying to keep that army of neighbors from trooping through there, invading her space. Nan requires a lot of space. If Ruby down at the store has a chicken that doesn't have those big nasty tumors of yellow fat hanging in under the skin, bring a good-sized one. Something green for a salad and a bag of those cashews. And wine. Red wine."

"Red?"

"Nan likes a good, strong red. Maybe Zinfandel. Check where it's from. The Sonoma Valley is fine."

If Ruby at the general store recognized him, she

didn't indicate it when he went in. But when he asked to examine the second chicken, she laid it out on waxed paper on the meat case and snorted. "Nobody's as picky about chickens as that Ash Porter."

While she added up the tab, Luke studied the candy display. The penny candy was all a nickel now except for the licorice whips, which were three for a dime. As he handed her the money he noticed she had set two cans of condensed chicken broth beside the things he'd asked for.

"Ash will need the broth for that rice he fixes with nuts," she told him, catching his glance. "He always forgets, and somebody makes another trip."

Luke chuckled. "You're way ahead of me. I didn't have any idea what he wanted these things for."

"Maybe we know each other too well up here. I know women who'd give a pretty penny to cook as good as Ash Porter does, myself among them. You must have taken up wine off in the army. Ash sticks with his Scotch."

Luke almost blurted out that the wine was for Nan Harrow. He caught himself in time. She looked up at him as she fitted the bills under the metal prong in the cash register. "You didn't go to Tom Harrow's funeral."

"I didn't know the boy."

She slammed the door shut and reached in the back of the candy case. "I used to think I did. But this past summer I haven't been so sure." Eddie Dodge had said Luke's timing was off, and Ruby was saying the same thing. To listen to Ash, the kid had been a problem from the first.

Ruby laid a red jawbreaker on the counter in front of him and grinned. "But I remember you." How could she remember one kid's taste after all that time? At his gesture, she shook her head. "My treat. You don't know how happy Ash's friends all were to see you come up here. It would be nice if you could talk some sense into him. But even lacking that, it's good knowing somebody gives a damn about Ash."

She read his thought and shook her head. "Having nobody but that Linden is worse than having nobody at all."

The aroma of Ash's meal cooking was enough to drive a man crazy for food. He *had* needed the chicken broth to cover the sautéed onions and rice. The sun was wholly gone, leaving a vague fused brilliance that turned the treetops into spiny silhouettes. Bandit made a sound in his throat, a deep, hungry sound without threat, as he thundered off the porch to disappear into the trees beyond the cabin.

"That's Nan coming," Ash said. "Bandit always hears her before I do. You might go meet her," he added.

"Good God, I've never met the woman."

Ash stiffened to stare at him. "She's our guest."

Luke's eyes took a moment to adjust after the brightness of Ash's kitchen. He followed the direction Bandit had taken along a rough path that led off behind the cabin. Nan Harrow and Bandit came into view almost at once, the small, solid woman with the shaggy dog keeping step under her hand. She was in jeans with low, rough boots. The plaid flannel collar of her shirt was almost buried by her loose, shoulder-length hair. He would have known her by the walk, very straight and light but purposeful. She paused when she saw him. Her face changed into something that was less than a smile, maybe a recognition. "Ash sent you out to meet me."

At his nod, she glanced up at him. "Once a father, always a father." Her hand was small, broad, and a little rough in his own. "I've looked forward to meeting you, Luke Adams. God knows I've heard enough about you."

"Those are always terrifying words," he said. "Look, Mrs. Harrow . . . "

"Nan," she corrected him.

"Nan," he repeated. "About today . . . "

She shook her head. "Don't say it for *me*, Luke. If you need to say it for yourself, go ahead. But I understand."

He hadn't known the difference until she defined it. "I need it for myself," he said. "I'm sorry."

She nodded formally and began walking again.

After a moment she looked up at him, her eyes studious on his. "If you don't mind, let's try to keep Ash from talking about the funeral. He needs to get his mind off it."

"What about you?" he blurted.

She stared at him. "He didn't say anthing about what happened there at the cemetery?"

"He sent me off for groceries. What happened?"

She stopped and looked down, stubbing the toe of her boot in that dark fan of earth where the drainage from the bee's water kept the dirt spongy and damp. "There was talk about who did it, and the robbery motive. Burt Roberts asked if Tom's camera had been found." She tightened her shoulders and started on. "Sheriff Dodge shook his head and said something about a camera being nothing, that it was money the thieves were after. Roberts argued, saying a seven-hundred-dollar camera was enough to tempt many a man to robbery."

She didn't need to say the rest, and Luke didn't want to hear it. Roberts was the same as accusing Ash Porter of causing the boy's death.

"Nan," he said, having a sudden problem with his voice. "Listen, Nan . . . "

She shook her head. "That's why I promised to come tonight, so Ash would know I knew better." She looked toward the porch, where Ash waited in the door, impatience in every line of his body. She left Luke's side and went swiftly up the stairs. When she leaned to press her face against Ash's, his hands caught her shoulders with a clawing desperation. Bandit circled, whining with frustration. Luke caught his ruff and tugged it hard, something like envy sour in his mouth.

Chapter 5

At first Luke was inclined to credit the strangeness of that evening to the Zinfandel. Ruby at the general store had guessed wrong. Except for a few disillusioning experiments in Europe, Luke had remained, perhaps in an unconscious aping of Ash Porter, strictly a whiskey man.

Before tackling the salad, Ash set out sturdy glasses with ridges down the sides. By the time Luke had opened the wine, Nan had solemnly arranged the hot dishes on Ash's table, civilized for the event by a cloth spattered with pale-blue daisies. Luke recognized the entree as a bastard coq au vin, ruddy onions nudging the wine-flavored chicken off its bones in a dark sea of fragrant sauce. The rice would have been meal enough alone, dense and moist, studded with a crisp astonishment of cashews.

Nan's hands were childish, short and broad with nails cut straight across, as if making a statement. She lifted her glass the same way she walked, purposefully, folding her fingers solidly around its thickness. She idly traced the ridges in the glass even when she wasn't holding it, even when she caught Ash's eyes and held them, forcing his conversation away from the day just past with a tactful stubbornness that amazed Luke.

Less than a week before, Luke had watched Linden's

slender fingers careful on the stem of a goblet. The wine had been very pale, not so much white as greenish in tone, as fragile and gleaming as the crystal it swirled in. Linden had ordered the wine with frowning care, then nodded to have his glass served. And he hadn't drunk it. In retrospect that had seemed churlish.

Watching Nan across the narrow table, he felt better about that decision. Damnit, he had contacted Linden assuming in confidence she would be, in spite of the rupture between them, as concerned as he was to make Ash both safe and happy. To realize that she didn't care about either of those things was still an astonishment. The memory of those dark eyes closed against him still rankled. Nan was as natural as Linden had been mannered and aloof, as giving as Linden had been self-protective.

Even with Nan's attention fixed intently on Ash, Luke drank eagerly of the same wine that had left a faint line on the down of her upper lip. Her determined efforts to avoid discussing the unpleasantness at her son's funeral were thwarted in the end by Ash. "A lot of nerve that Burt Roberts has," Ash said, his voice rising.

"He's not worth your anger," Nan told him.

"He's old enough to know better," Ash fumed, ignoring her. "Coming to the church tricked out like a parade horse, damn near burying that coffin in flowers, and then starting that business about the camera. You'd think he'd have more to do than come to a funeral just to raise a fuss about another man's business."

"No one pays any heed to Burt Roberts," she said. "Let me pass you something. Salad? Chicken?"

"Look who's passing," Ash grumped. "You've only pushed your food around. You best eat up yourself, or I'll make you take it home."

"Be careful, or I'll let you," she said, her mouth

tightening toward a smile. "And I might take yours, too, if you don't clean your plate."

Tom's name was not spoken. Neither was Will's. An inchoate anger swelled in Luke that this Will Harrow, this paragon Ash had bragged about, lacked the common decency to be at his mother's side.

As if he had summoned her thought, Nan turned to him.

"I'm glad you are here," she said.

"I told him to stay away, that it wasn't a good time," Ash put in.

"You've been wrong before."

"And so have you, young lady. And you're being wrong again if you think I'm going to let you go back through those woods to that empty cabin. Who knows what half-crazed man might see your shadow pass and fire willy-nilly? I have it all figured out. Luke here will bunk in the spare room and you use his place."

She shook her head and glanced at the Seth Thomas. "You know better than that, Ash Porter. And it's time I took off."

"At least let Luke drive you," he insisted.

She looked at Luke again, squarely. The warmth of the room had brought color to her cheeks, and her eyes, framed by dark lashes, were speculative. "California drinking laws are downright punitive," she announced.

"Good Lord, woman," Ash exploded with irritation. "Are you saying I raised up a boy that can't handle a few miles of mountain road with nothing but a glass of festered grape juice in his belly? I take that personally."

She chuckled deep in her throat and touched his hand with hers. "Festered grape juice, is it? You're lucky I don't take it home with leftovers."

"Be my guest," he said. "Luke, package up some dinner and put in some of the apples off the porch.

God only knows when this woman's had wit enough to lay in supplies."

Luke heard them talking quietly while he followed Ash's directions. When he returned, Nan had risen and was waiting for him. With the mountain road still to drive, Luke hoped the strangeness was not all Zinfandel. He had the distinct feeling that much had passed between Ash and Nan in those few minutes of his absence. Ash's expression was suspiciously innocent, and Nan seemed relieved of more than what had swelled the empty knapsack she lifted off the chair.

"Now, you be careful," Ash called after him. "All Eddie Dodge needs on you is a DUI."

She must have made some conversation on that trip to her cabin, which lay a mile or so north of Ash's place. For the life of him, Luke couldn't remember what they talked about. It had to be the wine that made him conscious of her in the seat beside him that his mind could absorb nothing more. When she told him where to stop, he was suddenly infected with Ash's paranoia. "I'll just carry these things inside for you and see that everything's all right."

The suggestion startled her into swift refusal. "No. You mustn't do that. It's fine. I'll be fine."

"At least let me carry them to the door for you."

She had the food containers in her hands, the sack of apples under her arm, and was out of the car in a wink. "Really, Luke. It's fine."

"Well." He turned firm. "I'm not leaving until you get a light on and wave me from the door that it's okay."

"You *are* Ash's son," she said, a smile in her voice.

"I will see you again?" he asked, struck by an unreasonable panic.

"Of course! Now, good night, and thank you."

Her silhouette against the lighted doorway looked small and painfully vulnerable. Too swiftly it diminished and then vanished as the door swung shut. He cursed as he backed out and turned to drive home.

Ash, with Bandit under his hand, called from the dark of the porch as Luke got out of the car. His pipe glowed and dimmed rhythmically as Luke approached. "Don't tell me you've cleaned up that dinner mess already."

"Very well, I won't," Ash replied. "You know she's seven years older than you if she's a day."

Luke stiffened against the words. "What's that supposed to mean?"

"Oh, hell, Luke. I'm crippled, not blind. It must be a long time between women for you to go down that hard."

As a man Luke had spent too much time with strangers to remember how transparent he was to Ash. And he had also been spoiled by having other people keep their mouths off his private business. Bands of muscle tightened along his throat, altering the timbre of his voice. "Listen, Ash," he began. His anger was as transient as it was swift. What was the use? "It's a long time for any man between women like that one."

When the bowl of the pipe only continued to pulse with sporadic light, Luke challenged the silence. "No answer to that, have you?"

Ash wheeled to the edge of the porch, braced his chair against the post, and knocked his pipe out onto the stone slab beside the ramp. Pricks of light winked and died among the tobacco ash. His wheels creaked a complaint from the wooden porch as he turned toward the door. "Tomorrow we better work the bees before some other damned thing happens."

The mystery of Nan's empty knapsack was partially solved over breakfast coffee. "I need a hiding place," Ash told Luke. "Not deep, but twelve inches, maybe, by about ten across."

When Luke glanced around the room, Ash shook his head. "Outside," he said. "This place is no more fire-safe than the next one."

"You must have a bank box," Luke said.

"Hell yes, I've got a bank box, and you're signed on it in case that ever comes up."

"How can that be? I never signed anything."

"I did," Ash said, his tone heavy with irritation. "What I want hid has to be buried, and somebody beside me has to know where it is."

Luke sighed. "You know this place better than I do anymore."

Ash nodded and launched into what at first seemed to be one of his spectacular non sequiturs. "The thing about the bees is that folks generally are terrified of them. Maybe you could dig me a hole between the hives. The ground's friable there from cultivation to keep the weeds and grass down."

"Ash," Luke protested. "There's the barn and the other cabin."

"All made of pure asbestos, I guess?" Ash asked.

It was damned awkward to wield a shovel in full bee-tending gear. Luke's sweat rose under the heavy veiling of the bonnet, coursing in rivulets behind his ears and down his chest. Ash's Wellington knee-high boots were a conspiracy against bending to the weight of a loaded shovel. When the hole looked deep enough and the right size, he straightened painfully and went up to the house. "Now what?"

Ash, who had watched from inside the screen door in case the bees took umbrage, handed Luke a package wrapped in oiled paper and tied with a cord that had plainly seen service as a wash line. Ash's phone was ringing as Luke set off across the clearing to bury the bundle and stamp down the dry earth above it.

The phone call was the first of several. There'd been

72

a lot of talk down at Maude's Place about the Boniface family's being farmed out here and there, without even a change of clothes to their backs. Maude was half-hosting a money-raiser. The beer would be at cost, and she was throwing in a pig to barbecue on the spit out back. "Somebody's bringing venison chili," Ash reported. "It's a buck a head plus whatever you can afford for the pot. And live music thrown in."

"How much money can they expect to raise that way?" Luke asked. The mountain economy he remembered had run more on barter than bucks.

"More than they'll have without it," Ash replied. As he spoke he wheeled to the kitchen and hefted a stew pot off the shelf. "I told Evie I'd put together baked beans for twenty or so."

"I'm not staying home this time," Luke told him.

Ash turned, studied him a moment, and then laughed. "Does that ever sound like the old days! Cut it out and go check the bees. You're overage in grade to sulk."

Luke felt his pulse quickening as he inserted the hive tool and lifted the top cover from the end hive. A man should handle bees all the time or stay away from them. He was as timid as he had been the first time he tried this process with Ash watching silently from a distance. He studied the bees running around over the space over the frames until he spotted the dark, slender queen. To his relief, she scrambled back into the hive.

Whoever had been keeping these bees knew his business. Slowly and methodically he inspected the frames, brushed the bees from the top storage box, lifted it off, and replaced the cover. When he turned with his smoker to approach the second hive he saw Nan Harrow watching him from the edge of the woods. She smiled silently and circled the cabin from the back to find a devious path toward Ash's door. Watching her go, he wanted to follow her as much as he wanted to stay away from her and Ash together. Thanks to Ash's infernal candor, it would push him to be natural with her now in the old man's company. And Ash was the one who had blown up about Burt Roberts's talking about other men's business!

To his relief, she stayed. When he had set the honey frames in the bee room and stripped off his gear, he found Nan and Ash studying a list at Ash's table.

"We need supplies," Ash said as Luke entered. "Nan wants some stuff of her own, if you don't mind her going along."

Luke nodded, avoiding Ash's eyes. "Fine. What about the honey?"

"Will rigged my extractor so I can run it from this chair," Ash told him. "I can get the most of it worked before you two get back." Luke groaned to himself. How was he going to rock a man loose who was this carefully and firmly entrenched? Ash handed him the list with a wad of folded bills. "Who knows? I might even get a nap in."

In the sunlight Luke noticed again what had struck him that day of the inquest. Nan's hair was at least three different shades of gold to brown, as if the sun had claimed what it touched and fought for more. She sat angled a little in the seat to talk to him, her eyes thoughtful on his face. "This is not much of a holiday for you."

"I'm not complaining yet."

She nodded. "I really am glad you came. You can't imagine how much Will and I have worried about his safety up here alone. Not only that, but I think Ash gets lonely. He likes people around."

"He told me how good you and your son were to him after his accident. You have my thanks for that, you know." When she nodded instead of speaking, he was disappointed. "What really happened in that accident, Nan? Linden told me the truck was at high speed and a stray bullet got the windshield. The part that didn't hang together was what the driver did afterward. Linden said he threw a big fit down at Maude's and then just took off. Those were her words."

Nan's eyes were on him, but her mind was clearly somewhere else. "It's interesting to hear the story told that way. As for speed, they all go fast. That's how they make their living. As for Ford throwing a big fit at Maude's, it seemed like more than that. The man was on fire with anger and pain. It was May, you know, and something was going on down at the high school. My boys and I had stopped in to eat before we dropped Tom off at his school for the evening.

"I hadn't heard anything about any accident until Ford lunged through those double doors. He staggered straight to the bar and started pouring it down. Right away a bunch of men gathered around. I still didn't know it was Ash he hit: I didn't find that out until late that night. But Ford was out of control, shouting, crying, threatening, clearly hysterical. He kept going back to that windshield shattering right in his face. 'I'll get the bastard that fired that bullet at me. I know where I was and where he had to be. I'll get that bastard if it's the last thing I do.' "

"Then it was just Ash's bad luck to be on that road."

"More than a combination of bad luck and fixed routine. The accident happened about four in the afternoon, the same time Ash always set out for Maude's Place to sit and jaw with his friends."

"What did he do then, just walk out and disappear?"

She nodded. "That would have surprised me more if I hadn't seen how badly he was blown away by what happened. I figured the company would settle him down, get him to a doctor for tranquilizers or some-

75

thing. As the boys and I were leaving in our car, one of the company men was walking him out, talking a mile a minute and tugging him along. He was quieter already, at least listening."

"Was that Roberts?"

She shook her head. "It was his assistant, the man Bo Sanders replaced. There was a lot of talk about how Eddie Dodge should have held Ford that night, but nobody thought of that until they found out he was gone." She glanced up. "I didn't know the man at all. He was somebody Roberts brought in from outside. But I still feel bad when I think about him going off like that carrying all kinds of guilt. The worst was that he and Ash had been halfway friends. He used to pull in and drink coffee with Ash and sometimes buy a jar of honey. I figured he couldn't stand to hang around and see Ash messed up like he was."

After working their way down both Ash's list and hers, they had coffee and a sandwich in town. "Surely you don't manage that mountain without a car?" Luke asked her.

She smiled. "It can't be done. Will's using mine. That's why I appreciate your hauling me around so much."

What prevented him from asking where in hell Will was? For one thing, he never got the chance. She was even more expert than Ash at changing the subject without warning. She leaned back in her chair and looked at him. "When I lived in that cabin I thought a lot about your mother." Luke looked up, startled. Nan couldn't possibly have known his mother.

"From what Ash said, we had a lot in common, your mother and me," she went on. "Both of us coming up there to have a good place to watch over our kids. I was just luckier than she was."

"I don't remember her," Luke said. "Nor my father, either."

She nodded. "My kids don't remember their dad. He was killed in a construction accident the year after Tom was born. Will was going on four."

"When I was a kid I used to wonder what happened to Linden's mother," Luke told her. "For some reason I was scared to ask."

"She left Ash," Nan said, her voice suddenly taking on a harsh edge. "Just up and left him, with Linden only a toddler." She shook her head. "I still see women do that and I shrink for my sex. It's too unnatural for me to understand. A mother watches over her kids"— the pause was minute—"as long as she can."

It was his turn to change the subject, and he managed it somehow. Damnit, Ash was too simplistic. Just because you found a woman fascinating didn't mean you were getting involved with her. But Nan did fascinate him. He wanted her to talk, to move, to eat, to breathe with that swift intake of air she did just before she spoke. He wanted to keep her talking until she had no more secrets from him behind that unlined forehead that glistened a little from the heat. Just being interested didn't mean what Ash had implied in his scathing comment. He didn't realize he was saying the words until they were out. "You are not an ordinary woman, Nan Harrow," he told her.

She flattened her square hand on the table and made that straight line with her mouth. "And I wouldn't call you an ordinary man, Luke Adams." The mock formality of her tone lightened the words.

"You don't know me."

"I know the Luke Adams Ash talks about. Then I know the one I see. That has to be at least a half-rounded view of you. I'll gamble on the rest."

They were halfway back up the mountain when they saw the plume of smoke rising on the slope above them.

Nan inhaled sharply and groped for Luke's arm. "Oh, my God," she breathed.

He closed his hand over hers. "Hey, hey. It could be nothing."

She drew her hand away at once and sat tensely beside him as he gave the car all the gas he dared. Since the smoke still rose north of Madrone, he turned in toward the town. A woman stood in front of Maude's staring at the smoke.

"What's on fire?" Luke asked.

The woman turned, looked at him, and then at Nan in the car. "A stable," she told him. "It was empty, thank God, not even any horses."

"Anybody know what started it?"

"Like they'll *ever* know," she replied, turning away to stare again.

"A stable?" Nan echoed. "They're sure?" She was coiled tightly in the seat with both hands pressed against her face, her body trembling wildly. "They're sure?" she repeated in a tone that edged toward hysteria.

He slid in beside her and caught her shoulder. "Nan," he pleaded. "There was nobody in it; nobody died. There weren't even horses."

She slid her hands down to stare at him with her eyes streaming. He could see her muscles relax even though the trembling was slow to pass. "I'm sorry I flew out like that. I can't think what got into me."

"It's not like you have been under a strain, or anything like that," he said, backing the car around.

Her tone was almost amused. "There for a minute you even *sounded* like Ash Porter."

That time Nan at least let him carry half the grocery sacks to her door while she hauled the others. "You have a big appetite for a little woman," he teased her. She flushed, set down the grocery bags, and turned to him with her back against the closed door.

"Thanks again, Luke." Then, with one of those swift

turns of mood he was just learning, her face puckered in annoyance. "Listen to me. That's all I say anymore. Thanks, Luke. Thanks, Luke. You don't owe me anything, Luke Adams. You haven't any call to do one thing after another for a practical stranger. How come you're doing all this?"

When the truth can't be said, try kidding. "Maybe I was just raised up right."

She spoke slowly. "I don't think that's all, Luke Adams," she said quietly. "But don't do *that* to yourself. Ash was right; you shouldn't have come up here. This is not over, Luke. It's not even half over."

"It's too late. I'm here. On both counts it's too late."

Her tears began again swiftly, and she covered her face with her hands as she had earlier. He took her in his arms hard, not so much holding her as bracing her against that awful trembling that racked her whole frame. Her body felt as solid as it looked, with firm, rounded muscle tone. Her hair smelled like pine. She didn't pull free, but the trembling stopped almost at once. She stood there in the shelter of his arms without moving. When she finally stirred, she looked up at him and wiped her cheeks with the backs of both hands. "It was seeing that fire," she said, her voice distorted by tears. "But it's okay now."

Then her lips drew tight again. "If you think I am going to say 'Thank you, Luke' one more time, you're crazy." She stretched and touched his mouth with the faintest brush of her lips. "Now go."

A huge center slice of ham was simmering on the back of the stove when Luke got home. The sweet smell in the air would be yams baked in their skins and bursting to be buttered.

"Did you hear about the stable fire?" Luke asked.

Ash nodded. "I saw the smoke and called Evie. She'd heard."

"If it's all right with you, I'd like a Scotch with dinner," Luke said.

"Pour two," Ash said. "Tough afternoon with Nan?"

"Not so tough as painful," Luke said, handing him his glass. "She went all to pieces when she saw the smoke of that burning stable up on the hill."

"That's not strange. Not after last week," Ash said. "It would have been strange if it hadn't scared her. It was up there not far from her own place. None of us want to see any more dying. Or burning either, as far as that goes."

Chapter 6

The money-raiser for the Boniface family was held in
Madrone on Saturday night. The street was already
lined with cars when Luke pulled in off the road. The
town looked different. He realized what was missing
at once. Both the ashes and the shell of the burned-
out building where Tom Harrow had died had been
cleared away since he had driven in with Nan on
Thursday to check out the smoke. Only a rectangle of
crumbling and smoke-stained bricks betrayed where
the garage had stood. After double-parking long enough
to get Ash and his chair out, Luke drove back toward
the highway, looking for a place to park.

He had stepped from the car and turned to pad his
hands against the heat of the roaster of hot baked
beans when he heard footsteps rattling the gravel along
the road behind him. The street light behind the man
threw his face in darkness. Not until Rick Boniface
spoke did Luke realize who had followed him.

"You've got guts coming here tonight."

"Hey," Luke said, straightening up and stepping
away from the side of the car. He wasn't going to take
on that much anger with his back against metal. "Don't
come on to me like that. I didn't fire your place."

Boniface didn't seem to have registered his words.
"You and Eddie Dodge! What's it costing you to buy

him off with those dirt samples from my place on the record?"

Luke sighed. "Give me a reason, Boniface, one shred of a reason I would try to burn you out."

"There *was* a man running." Boniface's tone was harsh. "He came from behind that garage streaking like a rabbit."

"What direction?" Luke asked. "Which way was he running?"

"East, across the road and toward the woods, toward that same place you appeared from only a few seconds later."

"Maude's Place is east and across the road. I had to circle that stinking mulch pile of hers to reach the road."

"But everybody at Maude's was accounted for. You were the only one with no reason to be there."

"A hell of a process of elimination. You like everybody's story but mine, so you eliminate them. Are all those people who were there at Maude's Place friends of yours?" A driver nudged his car down the road, drifting slowly to watch for a parking space. The flash of the car's headlights lit Rick's face for a vivid moment. What sounded like anger telegraphed fear in that brief light.

"Hell, no. I'm an independent, and no more a friend of Sanders and his toady than the next mountain man. But he was in the john. People saw him coming out."

"And I came out of the woods well after the explosion. I'd have never come into town if I hadn't felt that blowup and seen the fire. I wish to God I hadn't even stopped."

Boniface stood silent for a moment. "So what call did you have to be cruising along that road by my place that next morning?"

"I didn't have any call. I went where Ash directed me."

"What's Ash Porter lost over there?"

Luke groaned. "Get off it, Boniface. If you want to tangle with me, then let's tangle, and you take your chances. But lay off Ash. Ask yourself what Ash has lost and see what you come up with. That man grew up on this mountain, grew up and then got to be king of it. He was a faller, Boniface, a bull of the woods. You expect him *ever* to lose interest in the only life he had?"

A woman's voice was calling from down the road, a young voice shrill with concern. "That's Jenny," Boniface said. "I got to go." He paused. Luke felt him brace his fear with anger. "But watch it, Adams, watch it."

The couple preceded him up the road. Boniface's wife, under the loop of her husband's arm, was pressed so tightly against his body that Luke marveled she could walk. He thought of Nan.

Lanterns were strung between the lampposts in back of Maude's Place. The rich tang of seasoned pork layered the air and the music had already begun. Two fiddles, a guitar, and a set of drums were waging a losing battle against the cacophony of human voices rising and falling from the crowd clustered around the lot. Ash hadn't been the only one to get a call. A row of miscellaneous casseroles lined the table along with green salads, mounds of fresh-cut bread, and a lazy Susan of trimmings for the venison chili.

"I hope nobody saw you bring this in," Evie Hodges told Luke, clearing a place for the turkey roaster of steaming beans he had carried from the car. "Ash's reputation goes before him. Whatever Ash cooks is always cleaned out before I get a chance at it."

Groups had sorted themselves out. Luke looked around bleakly, wishing Nan had come. She had been adamant. "I'd only make it harder for everyone."

He would have argued with her if he hadn't thought she was right.

The appearance of a party didn't go any further than the lanterns and the display of food. No one was smiling. Except for quick gusts of laughter and shouting from a band of children racing in the woods, the voices vacillated between anger and frustration. A woman Luke didn't recognize passed from one group to another, officiously burdened with a clipboard.

"Petition," Evie Hodges explained. "Folks have written the authorities and got no response but form letters. A few folks have even gone down to the County House in Featherton and tried to collar people. Now we're going to officially request a hearing with the Board of Supervisors."

"What's supposed to come of this?" Ash asked.

"Protection," Evie said. "More police than just poor Eddie. Maybe somebody up from Sacramento. Good God, Ash." Her voice broke. "Two men have died. *Two men.*"

"I know, Evie," Ash said, his voice gentle as he reached for her arm. "At least a man and a boy." Luke knew Ash meant to be comforting, but Evie, tilted by her words over the frail edge of her control, nodded and turned away, fighting tears.

The woman with the clipboard approached, stared fixedly at Ash and Luke a moment, then turned away.

The last person Luke expected to see at the fundraiser was Burt Roberts. When the Robertses' sleek red sports car stopped in front of Maude's, he stared with the rest of the crowd. But Roberts's wife Amie, in riding pants and boots, jumped lightly out of the car and looked around as if confused.

Maude, just crossing the restaurant porch with an armful of condiments, stopped. "Looking for somebody, Amie?"

The girl walked to the foot of the stairs, looking up

at Maude with obvious relief. "I didn't know who was in charge," she said breathlessly. "Burt's gone on business." The listening of the crowd was so obvious that Amie Roberts moistened her lips nervously with her tongue. "If a person can't come to the dinner, is it okay to make a contribution anyway?"

As she spoke, Bo Sanders got out of the driver's seat and leaned on the roof of the car, listening.

Maude shrugged. "Nobody's really in charge, Amie. It's just a group effort. Sure you can contribute. Anything you give is going to be a help."

Amie held out a folded bill in her palm. After a moment's hesitation, she pushed it in Maude's apron pocket and smiled nervously. "I'm sure Burt would want to add to that, but you know how busy he is, and always away."

"Never mind Burt, thanks to yourself, Amie," Maude said. "Sure you won't stay for a bite? What you don't like you can always drown in ketchup." She glanced at Bo Sanders. "You're both welcome."

As Amie Roberts and Sanders left in a flurry of excuses, Ash prodded Luke with his elbow. "I never saw you before with your eyes on sticks."

"Get off that," Luke said. "It's just that every time I see that girl she gets prettier. But, my God, Ash, she looks no more than a child."

"Not every man is drawn to older women."

"Cut that out!" As Luke turned, he saw the twinkle of Ash's teasing expression, and relaxed.

"Amie *is* nice to look at," Ash admitted. "Bandit even likes her. But it makes me hopping mad that she has to be Burt Roberts's property. But a hell of a lot of folks around here are, whether they think they believe it or not."

"Now *that's* cryptic."

"Do you suppose another ten years in the army they could teach you another word?"

If Maude wasn't in charge, somebody pretty efficient was. When the crowd had been stroked down by music and softened by free beer, a middle-aged man managed to hammer a pot loud enough to get the crowd quiet. "We all know how little money any of us see up here," he said. "But every man has twenty-four hours in his day. We need a cleanup crew and a truck to haul the debris away." Evie made a list of those whose hands came up. "If you can swing a hammer, you can help get a new place framed in. Who do I see? Get those hands up."

When Ash turned and wheeled away, Luke followed. Maude came down the steps to meet him. "Trade favors with you, Maude," Ash said quietly. The rumble of requests for volunteers went on behind him.

"What's on your mind, Ash?" she asked, eyeing Luke as she spoke.

"You catch that big roaster I brought the beans in and hold it for me. In return, I'll stand for six windows in that new place of Boniface's."

"Why don't you speak out and tell them?" she asked, her tone brusque.

"Because I don't want to, that's why," he snapped. "I'm fagged, and my son is taking me back home."

"I've thought of a new word, Ash," Luke told him when the wheelchair was stowed in the car and Ash sitting beside him.

"So?"

"Curmudgeon," Luke said.

"That army may educate you yet."

The next few days passed lazy and relaxed, turning to a full week. A storm moved in from the Pacific bringing fresh rain to the mountains and evenings cool to keep the firebox in the kitchen burning days as well as evenings.

Nan came over to see Ash in midafternoon every

day. When it was around three, Luke set out toward her cabin to meet her halfway. About the time he crossed a certain logging road she would materialize out of the forest shadow, enveloped in a massive green poncho that belonged to Will. They walked back to Ash's together, often without even talking. Sometime during that week, without knowing when, Luke quit kidding himself about Nan Harrow's importance to him. But the old uncertainty remained, localized now into a pure terror that putting words on his feelings might endanger the delicate intimacy that fluttered between them.

She was the one who brought up the project that Ash had mentioned glancingly so many times. "Have you shown Luke the bird pictures?" she asked Ash.

"I guess I was waiting for the right time," he told her. "Maybe that's right now." He pointed to the bookshelf. "There, Luke, reach me down that big green album from the shelf."

"Like I told you before," he went on, with the book closed in his lap. "That good glass you sent me started the idea, that and what a good natural artist that Tom was. I couldn't believe how much difference the lens made in my seeing. A lot of the birds that were common when I was growing up are grown scarce, and I found myself wanting to see them in better color, their own color, and blown up as near full-size as possible. Since no grown man has time to wander woods like a boy does, I made this deal with Tom.

"A fellow down in Sacramento chose the camera and showed me what lens to buy. I couldn't believe the cost of that film, and it had to be sent off to a real photo lab for developing. But take a look at these."

Luke turned the pages in amazement. "My God, it's like a *National Geographic*. You mean that boy took all these pictures? They are wonderful."

Nan sat silent, her mouth set in that secret line.

"There was a lot of waste at the beginning," Ash admitted. "He'd get one or two good shots to a roll, but he worked at it and got better. Never went out without that Nikon swinging on his shoulder. Turn there to the back if you want to see a wonder."

These were night pictures, the worried stare of an owl peering through the darkness, the sweep of a hawk luminous in a moonlit sky. Luke whistled. "These are treasures."

"They ought to be, for what they cost," Ash said, his tone proud. "When we first decided to try night pictures, Mr. Patton down in Featherton told Tom and me about a special night camera called an owl camera. On his recommendation, we decided to forget that and go with a special night lens, along with special film. Those pictures take real slow to get the advantage of all the possible light. Since a man can't hold a camera still long enough for shots like that, we got Tom a tripod that folded and was easy to haul around. Hardly a day passes when I'm here by myself that I don't go through that book. I wouldn't take a fortune for it."

Luke noted Ash's careful handwriting beneath each picture. "There are two dates under every one."

Ash nodded. "There's the date I first saw that kind of bird, then the date Tom took the picture." He looked over at Nan staring silent into the fire, and his voice turned hearty. "What kind of a host am I? What can I get you, Nan, a pot of tea? A glass of wine?"

"Any of that Zinfandel left?"

Ash chuckled, wheeling toward the kitchen. "There's a fresh bottle, screaming to be uncorked."

Luke turned through the book again, this time more slowly. There must have been sixty plates. The earliest sighting date he found was April 23, 1924. The last picture in the book was dated May 15, 1985. Ash had been injured mid-May, 1985. He needed time to think about that. All that business about the boy going wild this summer past. Had Ash meant as much to Tom as he had to Luke himself? It sounded as though they spent a lot of time together, from the way Ash talked. Nan had said he was a baby when his own dad died. Maybe there was more to say for Tom than the mountain people had thought through. He felt Nan's eyes on him and closed the book to smile at her.

Luke hoped the rain might dampen the hysteria on the mountain. This hadn't been the first false hope he had ever entertained. Before any reply came to the petition, the next town meeting was called. Unless the venting of private fury in public served some viable need, those assemblies achieved nothing. Worse than that, they meant precious time he was losing with Nan. When Luke took Ash to the first of these, Nan agreed to come along. Luke watched her covertly in the rear-view mirror. She curled in the back seat with her chin resting on one hand and stared out the window. He wanted her beside him on the seat. But he always wanted her close. Looking at her made it easy to remember how it felt when she stood unmoving in his arms with her head fragrant against his chest.

Like Ash, she could read his thoughts. "You feel wary, as if you were waiting for something, or maybe were scared," she told him.

"All of the above."

"Because I am me or because I am a woman?"

Poor try at jesting. "You forget I'm a soldier. If you know where the fuse is, you can deactivate the bomb."

"You must know I'm not going to hurt you."

He had tightened his arms around her. He didn't know that. He didn't know any damn thing except that time had divided itself into two frightening dimensions; being with Nan and dreading their parting, and waiting to be with Nan, fearful lest that time not come.

But waiting was everywhere.

The tension should have eased as the days wore on without the outbreak of a new fire or the announcement of a new tragedy. Instead, the sense of hysteria rose steadily, almost impatiently. The papers reported a continuing rise in sales of guns and ammunitions. Notices of town meetings were posted everywhere. That Friday a slow rain was still falling after supper when Luke brought in a fresh load of firewood.

Ash shook his head. "Set it if you want, but don't light it. There's another town meeting tonight."

"I'm amazed you haven't had your fill of them," Luke told him.

"Maybe you had other plans?" Ash asked.

Luke was past dissimulating with the old man. "I don't care where I am as long as Nan comes along."

When Ash stayed silent and reached for his pipe, Luke challenged him. "What have you got against a man liking to be with a woman?"

Ash held his pipe firmly, but the match he scratched on the underside of the table danced in the air. "Why should I have anything against women? I had a wife. I even had a daughter."

Luke rumpled a sheet of newspaper from the yellowing stack by the stove. He laid the kindling twigs in a careful crossed design to give the damp cedar plenty of draft. Had he been home too long? He couldn't remember feeling such surges of irritation at the old man as he had in the past days. Cabin fever?

Ash's question had pushed past cryptic to irony. Sure, Ash had a wife, but she had run off, probably with another man, leaving him a toddler to raise. And Ash still had a daughter, whether he wanted to admit it or not. And she had "tangled" with him, whatever that meant, and left him, not to return even when he was crushed by forces more solid than disappointment.

"I never saw a man take so long to set a fire," Ash

said. The hard edge of his style rode too lightly on his words to make it through to his tone.

"I was thinking," Luke told him.

"Well you might," Ash said. "Very well you might. I've thought more on this than most men, I'd guess. If a man can think of any earthly way to live without a woman he dotes on, he should do it. And conversely, if a woman can take any joy outside of loving a man, she should, too."

Luke hesitated. He could banter with the old man. He could play Ash's own game and change the subject. Or he could be flat-out honest. "That's a darker side of it than I see," he said.

"That's your age talking," Ash said. "Not that I blame you. Nature confuses the young to keep new broods always coming on. We are set on the ground walking and right away we start dreaming of flight. Young, we fly into attachments. Old, we fly away from them. In the middle everybody preens and mates and scratches and gathers. But finally we all yearn to fly again."

This was the closest Luke had ever heard Ash come to talking about death. He should have grown accustomed to the old man's reading his unspoken thoughts, but Ash startled him.

"Not death," Ash said. "Pain. That second flight is away from the pain of attachment."

Only in the car on the way through the slow, darkling drizzle of rain did Ash move from the general to the specific. "Mind you, I got nothing against Nan Harrow. She's like a real daughter to me. But first off, she's a mother. Women who can be both wife and mother fall outside my experience."

The dark of the car was emboldening. "What about my mother?" Luke asked.

"The choice she made is clear enough. She came

up here to watch over you. The fact she didn't get to very long isn't her fault. Death has its own schedule."

"How do you know how she acted when she was with her man?" Luke challenged him. "You always said you hadn't met him."

"I never did," he said.

Ash's flat answer irritated him. "Dammit, Ash, that's no answer. My mother must have talked to you about him, some at least."

Ash nodded. "She did that, but all I know of him is what Belle told me. I don't want any man judging *me* by what Linden's mother gave witness of."

"That's fair," Luke decided aloud. He leaned to study the road ahead. The crowd had already gathered enough to fill all the space close up. He was going to have to let Ash off again and go find a place for the car. Distracted as he was, he almost missed Ash's quiet comment.

"Fair. When it's over, that's all I want them to say of me. Fair."

Now, that time he really *had* to be talking about death.

The air in the crowded room was dense from tobacco smoke and the moisture of the day-long rain. Luke found a seat at the end of a row, where Ash's wheelchair could sit beside him. He wished Nan had agreed to come with them.

"It's no use," she told him. "They aren't out to get to the bottom of this. They just want somebody to blame. If they can't blame a stranger like you, they'll pick on somebody else. I'm better off at home."

"You could at least stay and have supper with us," Ash had put in.

She shook her head. "I have lots of stuff up there, thanks to Luke taking me shopping."

Luke, watching the way she slid in under the straps of her inevitable knapsack, rose to walk her through the woods. There went his evening, right there.

The sheriff had chaired all the meetings before. The crowd stirred restlessly as the room filled and the designated hour passed without any sign of Eddie Dodge. The same broad man who had drummed up the volunteer help for Rick Boniface finally rose and went up front.

"Well," he said. "Looks like we're on our own tonight. Anybody know where Dodge got off to?" When no answer came, he posed a second question. "Did anybody talk to him about coming here tonight?"

A woman raised her hand. "He knew about it. I saw him in the store buying cigarettes about four. He couldn't have missed seeing the sign."

"But you didn't say anything?"

She shrugged. "Just that I supposed I'd see him tonight. He said he hoped so, but he had another meeting before that."

"Like any other meeting could be as important as this."

Another voice chimed in. "We might as well not have any law as have a man who hangs back from arrests."

"Now don't overstate things," the man at the podium coaxed. "The law can't make an arrest until it has a suspect."

Luke knew without looking that the man on his feet was Rick Boniface. "Don't put any money on that!" Boniface said angrily. "He's got himself a suspect. I saw the car license the night my place was fired. Even after Dodge found the car and the lab reports showed soil from my road on it, he's still hanging back."

Ash's voice broke in. "You know damned well my Luke didn't fire that house of yours, Rick Boniface."

"That's not the only thing," another voice spoke up. "What's he done about the robbery up at Tom Har-

93

row's, not even counting the fact the boy was murdered?''

"I know what that boy's camera was worth," somebody said. "That's way past petty thievery."

Luke felt Ash's anger vibrating the sleeve of his coat. When Luke laid his hand on Ash's arm and murmured, "Easy," the old man stared straight forward and shook his hand off.

The complaints voiced all over the room brought Burt Roberts to his feet. Luke turned at his voice. This was his first good look at Roberts since the inquest.

Burt had taken a seat against the back wall of the room. Amie Roberts, her slenderness belted into a pale trench coat spattered with rain, sat between her husband and Bo Sanders. She stared straight ahead, as if her mind were a million miles away. Having seen her tentative manner with Maude, it struck Luke that the girl was shy. Maybe her total absence of expression was a defense against the room of eyes turned on her husband and, of course, herself.

"Look, people," Burt Roberts said. "We all feel the same growing concern about what's been happening. But this talk is getting us nowhere. There's got to be a next step."

"Law," Rick Boniface said. "We need some law up here with guts."

Burt shrugged. "Maybe that's the answer."

"We've tried petitioning for more law," someone shrilled. "We got nothing, worse than nothing."

"Elected officials can be recalled," Roberts said mildly. Then he sat down.

"Petition," somebody called. "We can petition to have Eddie Dodge taken off our necks up here."

"And his books," someone added. "With all the taxes we cough up, I'd like to see his books."

The wording was hashed and rehashed until the petition was agreed on, to audit the sheriff's records and recall him for incompetence. Somebody had risen to suggest an addendum when the door burst open, sweeping the room with a rush of cold, wet air.

"Murder!" Silas Engel shouted from the doorway. "Bloody murder."

As the old man's voice trailed off, Luke turned to see Engel sway to brace himself against the side of the door. He was hatless, his long hair pasted to his skull by rain. He leaned to one side, hugging his left arm to his body as he struggled for balance. The same rain that had glued his hair down had diluted the blood oozing from between the fingers that gripped his bloody jacket.

"Murder," he wailed. "I been shot."

The room exploded with sound as men leaped to their feet, shouting. There were as many screams as tears from the women. "Come on, Ash," Luke whispered. "Turn this thing around and let's get out of here." Ash nodded and obeyed wordlessly.

Outside it wasn't really raining as much as drizzling, the air so heavy that it turned to water against his face. "Just brace me," Ash said. "I'll go with you to the car." Halfway down the road they could still hear the shouting inside the meeting hall.

"Poor Eddie," Luke said as he closed the passenger door beside Ash.

The old man sat silent as Luke started the car, turned the vehicle around, and drove toward the road. The silence was uncomfortable, heavy and painful.

"Back there I was thinking about flash points," Luke said. "I been raised hearing about flash points, knowing that the difference of a single degree in temperature stood between safety and something exploding into flame. Who would have thought that the sight of old Engel's blood would trigger a flash point in that crowd?"

"Men have them, too," Ash said quietly. "A man goes along thinking he's on top of his own nature.

95

Then something fires his flash point. I hope to God Eddie Dodge doesn't show his face until the fever goes down."

As they neared the general store, Ash asked Luke to pull in. "What do we need?" Luke asked.

"Scotch," Ash told him, struggling to wrest his wallet from his pocket.

"I'll get it," Luke told him. "I thought we had plenty."

"One man's plenty is another man's drought," Ash growled.

Ruby was stacking a shelf at the back with the radio blaring. She kicked the ladder away and came up front. "Town meeting over? They're quitting early tonight."

"Ash and I just took off," he told her, pulling the bottle from the shelf. "Silas Engel staggered in with a bullet in his arm and the crowd went crazy."

She stared at him a moment. "Silas is the crazy one. He's been asking for a bullet in those woods ever since I can remember. He was screaming for it, to go out at night as trigger-happy as these people are now." Her voice dropped with sudden repentance. "He's okay, isn't he?"

"Like I say, we left. Surely somebody was going to see to him."

She rang up the Scotch and handed him change. "Where's your lady friend tonight?" She met his glance levelly, daring him to contradict her. "Nan Harrow didn't go with you?"

"Maybe she's had enough of these useless drills," he told her.

"It's got to be tough for her right now. Losing one kid and having the other one off God knows where."

As irritated as Luke himself felt about Will Harrow's absence, he didn't like Ruby's attacking Nan's son. He wanted to protest her judgment, but let the moment go too long. "Well?" she challenged him. "You haven't seen Will Harrow around here, have you?"

Chapter 7

The only calendar in Ash's house was back in the bee room. It had come from a service station whose name Luke didn't recognize. Neither did he recognize the handwriting of the terse notations that recorded what care the bee colonies had gotten. It was clearly a man's handwriting, bold pen strokes, almost vertical except for a slight tilt to the left. From what Luke remembered hearing about graphology, those factors indicated a writer inclined to strong ideas and who kept his own counsel. Since the calendar entries had certainly been put there by Will Harrow, Luke glared at them every time he passed. If Nan's son had a strong mind, he wasn't using it, and if he was keeping his own counsel by letting Nan handle Tom's death on her own, he needed a better adviser.

Two and a half weeks had passed since the boy's death. He had watched Nan come lonely from the woods, and go lonely back home. Ruby had spoken of Will's absence. Ash had, too. Maybe Nan's talent as a state-of-the-art mother extended into the farther reaches of complete understanding. Only, Nan had said nothing about Will's being gone. How many times had he heard her say, "A mother watches over her kids"?

Mostly he avoided looking at that calendar at all. Back in Germany a month of leave had sounded like forever. Nan had changed that. With half his leave spent, the remaining days had picked up momentum, stumbling over each other in passing. And nothing had been solved on the mountain. Eddie Dodge was fighting for his job, loaded guns still leaned inside cabin doors, and Rick Boniface was trying to coerce everyone he could collar in joining his crusade to get Luke Adams behind bars for the public good.

All that was bad enough. Leaving Nan was the unthinkable part. The best he could do was live for the afternoons they spent together.

Ash seldom admitted that he usually dozed a while after lunch, but he did. He'd waken with a start, make a trip to the john, and start peering around at the clock to see if it was time for Nan to come by. In the end he would get impatient enough to bark at Luke. "For God's sake, go see what's keeping that Nan."

Luke knew what was keeping Nan. He had suggested that she wait there in the woods where he could meet her and walk her in. She had protested when he first came up with the idea. "I can't lie to Ash. I don't even want to."

"I'm not suggesting a lie," he told her. "I'm saying that we need . . . Anyway, I need at least a little time alone with you. Hell, Nan, it's not a lot to ask, just that I get to meet you and touch you before we go back to Ash."

She had leaned against him. "This is wild and insane and somehow dangerous."

He lifted her chin with a single finger and smiled at her. "Dangerous to whom? If Ash weren't such a rockbound old conservative he would understand and accept that a few years between us don't keep us from loving."

"We can't play that game every day," she countered. "Ash would figure that out fast enough. If I want you to come for me, I'll settle down by the path and wait for you."

"Anything to stay in control," he told her.

She shrugged and angled her eyes at him. "Maybe just keep you off balance."

If Ash suspected anything, he had kept his mouth shut.

That day it was Luke himself who got restless, eyeing the Seth Thomas with growing impatience. He rose, stretched, and announced he was going off to "see what was keeping Nan."

Bandit was trained far better than the average dog. Luke guessed Will to be responsible for that. When Bandit was told to sit and stay, he nearly bounced and wriggled himself to death, but he never left the spot. Luke, unwilling to share a shred of Nan's attention even with him, left him whining mournfully on the porch.

The bees had either figured out that he had robbed them or sensed the coming of winter in the cool rains. They were working harder than ever. He paused to watch an elaborate dance outside the last hive of the row. If he could remember the pattern until he got back, he could find that patch of bloom for himself from the diagrams in Ash's old bee book.

The woods had smelled different ever since the rains began, fresher and dustier both at once. Once in a while a breeze brought a whiff of cedar smoke from a newly fired stash pile somewhere on the mountain. He startled a jay and took a scolding before crossing the road to find Nan.

He knew she was in the woods before he could see her. He didn't understand that himself, but he was always right. He had told Nan early on that he always knew whether she was waiting for him or not when he left the road. She had scoffed at him. "There's no way you can see me from the road," she told him.

"It's not a matter of seeing," he told her. "The woods change when there's a human in them. Birds turn shrill from nerves and the rustling gets sly." She had made a soft sound in her throat like swallowed laughter. "You don't buy that?"

She shook her head, still with a half-smile. "If you're there to listen, there's already a human changing the woods."

She hadn't put it as a question, so he hadn't answered. Never mind how, he always knew.

At the turn of the path, he saw her. At first he thought she was sleeping against the base of the big fir. She was sitting curled, her back resting against the tree trunk and her arms looped around her legs. Her head was resting on her knees so that strands of that strange hair fanned over the faded blue of her jeans and concealed her face. He didn't even call out to her. He liked being able to look at her all of a piece like that without being distracted by her wide-spaced eyes looking back at him, studying him. He liked thinking of how putty-soft and slowly she wakened, dragging herself back to consciousness with her breath coming in short, shallow exhalations like sighs. For a moment there he was tempted to let himself down beside her to fit his body against her warmth. Instead, he kneeled and trailed a single finger across her forehead to lift the hair from her face.

Nan's head rolled to one side at his touch. All the way to the side. He felt something pass his lips, a grunt, a curse, he didn't know what, as her head, severed at the bubbling red line where her throat had been, came to rest on her left shoulder. Her eyes stared past him into the woods, past his shock and the sudden thundering pulse in his temples.

He staggered to his feet, unsteadied by horror, backed a few steps, then turned to run. He was nearly to the road when the roar of an approaching lumber truck brought him to a stop. He hunched silently in a grove of second-growth trees to let the rig pass. As the sound faded, he heard the faint, distant whine of a siren and felt his flesh crawl.

Then he remembered.

Someone had been alive in the woods when he came in. Someone besides himself. He had figured it was Nan and he smiled at knowing she was waiting, knowing that meant that in spite of her stinginess with words, she was as eager as he to steal what fugitive moments they could find alone.

But Nan was already dead when he got there.

The only person alive in those woods besides himself had to be the monster who had carved that neat line of death across her throat.

He stood and stared into the woods, his heart thundering against the hard knot of pain in his chest. No extra leaf stirred, no shadow changed, but someone was still alive in those woods besides himself, listening and waiting.

The siren drew closer. Luke turned and ran toward Ash's house, not even staying to the path, not even dodging the branches that slapped and clawed his streaming face.

His feet weighed at least a ton each, picking them up and laying them down. When he reached the edge of the clearing, he heard Bandit whining. The dog was still waiting on the porch, his lean rib cage thumping on the painted floor with eagerness.

"Okay, Bandit," he said, his voice thick and alien in his ears. The dog leaped into the clearing and landed running. His tongue, with its inexhaustible flood of slimy spit, washed Luke's hands all the way to the porch.

Ash wasn't waiting at the door; already that was strange. Ash always waited at the door to get the first sight of Nan coming out of the woods with that clean walk of hers, that walk that told the world she knew where she was going. Luke shoved the dog back and stepped inside. Ash was at his table, staring straight ahead into the woods. He didn't even look around. Luke paused, gasping around the growing weight in his chest to find wind to speak with. That was all right. Ash wouldn't have let him speak anyway. The old man lifted his right fist and brought it down on the table hard, like a man setting an ax into a green stump.

"Don't say a word," he intoned in a slow, steady rhythm. He paused only a single beat, then repeated himself with elaboration. "Don't say a goddamned word. I can't deal with words anymore." He whirled the chair so swiftly that Luke stepped back, bringing a whine of hope from Bandit, still pressed against the door. "They should have never scraped me off that highway and put me back together. I should have never let them string my nose to sugar like a babe too weak to suck. If I died, maybe she wouldn't have had to."

"There was somebody else there," Luke told him.

"Sure as hell there was," Ash exploded. "There was a damned traffic jam there. Bo Sanders was there. You were there."

"Bo Sanders?"

He nodded. "He called in to the sheriff's office on that radio in his car."

"And he saw me?"

"He couldn't have." Ash shook his head. "You hadn't had time to get there unless you flew. Eddie Dodge must have hung up on Sanders and dialed here without putting the phone down. He didn't tell me what was up; he only asked to talk to you." Ash stopped and fought for breath. "I told him you were meeting Nan Harrow in the woods."

"There was somebody else there," Luke repeated.

Ash just looked down at his hands, which must have been smarting from those blows on his table. "Dodge said for you to stay here if you came back. Her throat, Luke?"

"Her throat."

Ash turned back to his window and stared through it, past the sheared clearing and into the woods that were his life. "You never know what you've done until it's too late, Luke. I never knew I had taken me the wrong woman until she was gone and the shadow of her restless hungers darkened Linden's eyes. I never knew I had taken me a son until you came back too stubborn to keep failing and too proud to take help. I never knew . . ."

The whine of Eddie Dodge's siren overwhelmed Bandit's plea. Ash said, "Oh hell, what's the use? Once we know what we've done wrong, it's always too late."

Luke walked to the porch and called the dog off Eddie Dodge. Eddie stood beside the car looking at Luke. "You wasn't here when I called."

Luke nodded. "I had walked through the woods to meet Nan Harrow."

Dodge sighed. "I guess you know you're coming down to the office with me."

"I'm coming, too," Ash called from behind Luke. "Get my coat, and reach me the checkbook out of that drawer where I keep it."

"You might not have any way to come back home, Ash," Dodge told him.

"Then again I might," Ash said, closing the front door behind him.

"Who's with her?" Luke asked Dodge.

"I deputized Sanders," he said "The sheriff is sending a man up from Featherton with cameras and all."

Chapter 8

Luke tried to talk Eddie Dodge out of taking him down in the cruiser, but the deputy was adamant. Ash, triumphant at his small victory of being allowed to come along, was probably safer with Eddie driving anyway. Halfway down the hill, a billowing cloud of white smoke erupted from above the trees to the left and south of the road. Although it had to be a half-mile or more away, the scent of wood smoke flowed in through the open window of Dodge's car. Luke concentrated intently on the burgeoning smoke, trying to fill his mind with it, to blot out the vivid memory of Nan's head rolling lazily sideways at his touch.

Eddie Dodge peered into the mirror and caught his eye. "I know what that one is," he said. "I was notified they were going to burn that slash pile. We could still get a dry spell or two. There's a crew there watching it."

Ash grunted something unintelligible. Eddie glanced at him and fell silent. He turned off on the road to Madrone and drove past Maude's Place. The sheriff's substation was at the edge of town, a trailer up on blocks with a five-hundred-gallon gas pump set beside it. Eddie slowed down and cursed quietly to himself. Silas Engel had gathered a crowd on the vacant lot in front of the trailer. Although Engel's wounded left arm was tied close to his chest in a soiled makeshift brace, he was shouting and gesticulating with his one good arm. "Murder!" he yelled. "Bloody murder, and God's will be done."

Dodge was out of the cruiser instantly and at Engel's side, clumsy with annoyance. "Now look here, Silas," he said, taking the old man's good arm. "You don't want to be run in for disturbing the peace, do you?" Dodge fished in his pocket. "I'll stand you a beer over at Maude's. Just cool it. We've got serious business."

The old man jerked his arm away and struck Dodge's hand, sending the coins rolling. "Murder!" he cried. "Bloody murder, and God's laws avenged! The temptress lies dead." As Engel swatted at Dodge's attempt to restrain him, his voice deepened, taking on a ponderous rhythm. "In the end she is bitter as wormwood, and her feet go down to death."

Ash roared from the front seat. "Luke, get me that damned chair. Silas, you old reprobate. I'll shut you up!" He flailed helplessly behind his seat, groping for the wheelchair Luke had folded there.

"Now, Ash," Dodge called to him. "You know how Silas is. Pay him no mind. You stay in there until I get—"

"Luke, dammit, get me that chair," Ash howled, ignoring Dodge. "Know how he is! Everybody up here knows he's bonkers. That gives him no license to vilify Nan."

"A man without sense," Silas screamed back at him. "All of them, all her men. Like birds into snares, down to the chamber of death."

"Give me a hand here," Dodge shouted to the men gaping around them. "Pitch in and help."

"If I only had my legs," Ash moaned. "If I only had my legs, I'd shut that filthy mouth of his." By the time Luke got the chair in place with Ash into it, Engel was being hauled down the road, still shouting.

Dodge seized the back of Ash's chair. "Straighten up, Ash Porter," he snapped at him. "Good God, all I need is you two old idiots trying to kill each other."

Luke followed numbly as Dodge wheeled Ash to the door of the trailer and tilted him up the makeshift stairs and into the untidy office. The windowsills were golden with drifted pine pollen and the floor streaked with boot marks. The room reeked of stale strong coffee and trapped smoke. Eddie had his sleeves rolled up above his elbows. The hair on his arms swam in sweat as he leaned on his desk and shoved an overflowing ashtray to one side. "All right, Adams. Give me your story."

"He doesn't have to say a thing without a lawyer," Ash snapped.

"Come on, Ash," Dodge pleaded. "I just need to get this square in my head. You didn't see me hauling Luke down to Featherton, did you? You don't see anybody taking this down, do you? You don't see my writing things for Luke to sign. I just want to know what in hell happened and when."

Luke stared at him. Nan. Nan was what had happened. Dodge's tone softened, "Look, Luke. An investigator is probably already working up there by now. They're going to go over everything, shred by hair. I'll be meeting Doc Meyers down at the mortuary for an inquest. Maybe he can even fix a time of death. I need some kind of frame to put this in. What time did you go off to meet Nan Harrow?"

"Not even five minutes before you called, Eddie Dodge," Ash broke in.

"You really want me to put you and that chair outside till this is over, Porter?" Dodge challenged him.

"I don't know the time," Luke admitted. "It was after three-thirty. She usually came over about then."

"But you went to meet her today?"

Luke felt his flesh redden. "I often did that." There

was nothing to tell but the truth, and he told it, over and over, as he had been pressed to do the day Tom Harrow died.

"You keep saying somebody was in the woods," Dodge said. "It couldn't have been Sanders. He saw her and ran out to the road on the other end of that section to call me. You must have seen somebody to know they were there."

"I saw no one," Luke repeated. "But somebody was there. Engel." He thought suddenly. "Who told Silas Engel Nan was dead?"

Dodge studied him a moment, frowning. Then he rose. "Help yourself to that stale coffee back there and I'll go try to get some sense out of him. Use the powdered cream even if you don't want it. That coffee's got to be a hundred proof by now."

"What in hell did Nan ever do to anybody?" Ash asked. His words echoed bleakly in the quiet room as Luke went to pour them each a cup of coffee.

Dodge dragged himself back and slammed the door hard behind him. "Luke Adams, I never saw a man so intent on making himself look bad. Everybody on this mountain knew Tom wasn't cold before you and Nan started carrying on."

Luke didn't realize he was on his feet until Ash caught his arm and pulled him back down.

"Should have put that different," Dodge mumbled. "But it was common knowledge, Luke. Lots of talk. Now she's dead. And yet, I'll be damned if I can see my way clear to holding you with what Silas is saying. He says there's more than one of you coming and going from that cabin of hers, and at all hours, too."

Sick. If he didn't let the anger loose, Luke was going to puke all over that cluttered desk already glistening with sheriff sweat. Too many swift images flashed at Dodge's words. Nan's insistence that he never go into her house. Nan, her back firm against the closed door, facing him. Nan and her loads of groceries, more than he and Ash could use in a week.

"So maybe that's why you should hold me," Luke told him. "Maybe I got tired of being only one in her crowd. Jealous rage, is that what you want? That old fool Engel hasn't lost his cow, he's lost his marbles."

"Be grateful for the old cow Boss," Dodge said. "Engel is in those woods all the time. He may throw more scripture in with the truth than we want to hear, but he sees what he sees. Men who believe in the kind of God Silas does don't make a practice of lying."

Luke looked at him, swallowing hard against waves of nausea. "You two come on," Dodge said. "I'm releasing you on your own recognizance, Luke Adams. You know better than to leave as well as I know better than to do this." He rose and glared at Luke. "They're going to get my head for this, you wait and see. They're going to chew me up and spit me out so small a hawk couldn't find me. I'll be honest. When I brought you in here, I meant to charge you. I didn't have one single other thing in my mind. But I can't do it in good conscience with what Engel is saying. Come on. I'll drive you back up the hill and see how the investigator is coming along."

A number of men and women waited across the street, watching. One of them shouted at Dodge, an epithet Luke didn't catch. "Go home," Eddie called back. "There ain't any party." Behind the sound of Dodge's motor starting, Luke heard an angry voice shout a slogan he hadn't heard since coming home. "The U.S. army trains killers."

It was silent in the car going up the hill. Dodge pulled in close to the porch to make it easy for Ash. "Hold yourself ready for a hearing tomorrow," he told Luke. He paused. "If you got any ideas on how to locate Will Harrow, I'd appreciate the help. I'll go through her cabin after a bit, for all that's worth."

Ash wheeled through the door and went straight for his table. The afternoon had wasted him. His flesh had pasted itself closer to his bones, throwing his nose and eye sockets in craggy relief. He reached for the binoculars and closed his hands around them tight. He half lifted them, then remembered. "We're going to have to think about supper, I guess."

Luke shook his head. "Later I could scare something up. You missed your nap, you know."

Ash bridled automatically. "Nap!" Then he slumped. "You know I don't take naps. Anyway, with the sun behind the hill, it's already dusk. But you could set a Scotch over here for me before you leave."

Luke lifted out two glasses and then put one back. Bandit whined from the porch as Luke set the drink beside Ash. "Okay," he told the dog. "So you're hungry."

When he carried the bag of dog food out to refill Bandit's dish, he realized Ash was right. The woods were dark with twilight and a few pale stars struggled to visibility through the deepening color of the sky. The trembling seized him without warning along with the swift flood of burning tears. The last day of Nan's life was gone. After he set Bandit's bag of food back into the pantry, he pulled Nan's bottle of Zinfandel out from under the sink to take back to the cabin with him.

Smelling the pipe smoke from the center of the clearing raised a fine brush of hair on the nape of Luke's neck. That wasn't Ash's Durham, and Ash hadn't even reached for his pipe. He had two choices, to walk straight across that clearing or take a devious route, stealthily from tree to tree, until he could see whose pleasure was being carried fragrant on the wind. But it *was* his cabin, and he never knew a man with less to lose than he had. He walked straight across the middle of the clearing, even though it meant he was fully exposed every step of the way. As he passed the beehives he saw the figure of a man in the shadow of that blooming vine. He was leaning back against the closed door, waiting.

"Well, anyway, you got guts," the voice spoke from the shadow. "If I'd have wanted to nail you, I had a half-dozen chances." His tone was more amused than threatening, a young voice, slurring the words, mountain-style.

"Why would you want to do that?"

The man stood up straight, the pipe loose in his right hand. He was average-sized, heavily bearded, with a barrel chest above lean hips. "Will Harrow here. The word is that you killed my mother."

Luke's anger rose as quickly as his mind credited what he had heard. He held it out of his voice as best he could. "And you don't think so?"

"You could convince me," Will said with a note of invitation. "On the surface, I can't imagine why."

"Maybe we should go in," Luke suggested. "In case Ash raises his glass at that window."

"When he's hurting, Ash doesn't look out, but in," Will told him, stepping aside to let Luke enter before him.

"There's coffee," Luke offered. He lifted the bottle he was carrying. "There's even red wine, if that's your pleasure."

"Coffee's fine." Will nodded. "But after a bit. I want to hear your side of this story."

"And I want to hear yours, dammit." Luke exploded without knowing it was coming. "The hell Nan has been through these past weeks. And alone!"

"She had you." Will's voice was level. "She was calling all the shots herself, the whole time."

Luke looked at Will Harrow in the lamplight. Like Nan's, his eyes were spaced a little far apart. His brows, darker than Nan's, met over the bridge of his nose, and his eyes were as level as his voice.

"I wasn't enough," Luke told him.

"Nobody would have been. Tom was her kid. But you were there, and in the right way. Like I said, I want to hear your side of this story."

Luke felt himself sag under the energy of this man's patience. "She came to Ash's afternoons. There was a place we used to meet on the way. When I got there, she was dead."

"You two were lovers?"

"What kind of a question is that?" Luke heard his voice rising but couldn't get it under control. "It's none of your damned business. But I loved her, if you're interested to hear that."

"Hey," Will broke in. "I guess I just wanted Nan to have had everything she's going to miss by dying too soon. And she was fair gone on you."

"How do you know that?" Luke challenged him.

"I could use that coffee now," Will replied.

Will was a leaner, as Nan had been. Arms crossed over that rounded chest, he rested his weight against the wall and watched Luke measure the coffee, fill the pot, and press the metal starter until a spark caught the gas, flared up a minute, then settled to blue jets.

"So who do you think killed her?" Will asked.

Luke sighed. "All I've done today besides fight the shakes is ask myself that. What I can't find is cause."

"What was the cause of Tom being killed?" Will asked. "He was little more than a kid."

"I figured it had something to do with all that money they found," Luke said. His words brought back Dodge's last remark. "The sheriff was going up to go through Nan's cabin."

"I figured on that." Will nodded. "I got my stuff out as soon as I heard. It's stowed up in the loft of Ash's barn."

"I'm missing something, Will Harrow. You had your stuff at Nan's? And how come you picked today to come back?"

"I've been back and forth the whole time. I was out of the state when they got Tom. Mom called me that night late. I wanted to start straight home, but she went all to pieces, begging me to stay away. When I reminded her I had work to do down here, she gave in but made me promise to hide out once I got here. I've never seen her that scared before, and it was too much, along with the grief."

Will's eyes were like Nan's, no particular color but flecked with brown under a blackness of lashes. At first Luke had thought she painted her eyes that way, but decided different when they were always the same, even when she was crying.

"Whoever killed her had to be mad. Only a madman kills without cause."

"Mad or angry," Will said. "He also had to be somebody she knew. Nan wasn't a woman to let just anybody get close to her. What else I heard was that you could use a friend on this mountain."

"I wouldn't argue that. Dodge is trying to be fair, but some of the others are out for my hide."

"I'm out for who killed Nan," Will said. "I've been two weeks now trying to get used to Tom being gone. I'm not ever going to get used to losing Nan."

"We've got that in common. Are you offering to be that friend?"

Will noded. "If Nan was right, I may need a friend as bad as you do. And Ash may need us both."

"Now what does that mean?"

"Ash has been real busy since that accident of his. He's ruffled a lot of feathers."

The plume of steam from the coffeepot smelled rich enough. Luke stared at it. He needed an eggshell to settle the grounds. He didn't have an egg. He shrugged and swung the pot a minute before he filled two mugs. Will's words had imprinted without registering. "Are you saying Ash Porter is behind all this stuff that's come down?"

Will had the mug to his lips, blowing on it. Nan's eyes looked back at Luke through the mist of steam. "Ash and Nan together have been poking at a hornet's nest for a long time. I've been party to a little of that myself. Once you start stirring things up, you're begging the other guy to make a move."

"Then you know who killed Nan?" Luke asked.

"I honestly don't. And knowing is only going to be half. We've got to prove it, too."

"Dammit, Will. Ash has nearly driven me out of my mind these past two weeks saying halves of things. I'm not in any mood to take it from you, too. Ruffled whose feathers? Poked at what hornet's nest?"

Will balanced his mug carefully and let himself down on the daybed. "Burt Roberts has been a thorn in Ash's craw ever since he slept with his daughter Linden for years and years before throwing her over for a rich man's daughter half his age or less." Will met Luke's eyes. "That can't be news to you."

"I was gone," Luke protested. "I only knew they fought and Linden took off. But that would explain . . ." There wasn't any point in rehashing the Linden who had been against the Linden who was.

"Ash settled all those years for the kind of simmering hate mountain men grow up on. He made no secret he thought Roberts was a crook, and a lowlife bandit raping everyone in sight. His words, I might add. Being crippled by that company truck changed all that. From the day he got back on this mountain he was out to prove Burt Roberts belonged in prison."

Luke whistled softly. "Dodge called it a feud."

"It looked like a half a feud until Jerry Hodges was

113

killed. And all this time Tom was going down the tube, from the very day Ash got hit."

"I have a theory about your brother," Luke volunteered. "Ash must have been all the father he ever knew. If anything had happened to Ash when I was growing up, I would have probably blown forty ways to Sunday, too. But I still don't see how Nan got involved in Ash's one-way feud."

Will shrugged. "I figured it was Tom and his money. Nan couldn't believe how that boy went out of shape. Even though Tom had a lot of trouble with Roberts when he was a kid, Nan couldn't think of anybody else who could be feeding that much money to the kid."

"Ash said Tom was working for *him*."

"He was, for a couple of years there. He took great pictures, and Ash paid him well. But Tom quit taking pictures when Ash got hurt. But he still had money coming in from somewhere, more money than we had ever seen."

"Roberts isn't one to pay out for nothing."

Will shrugged. "Crooks and lowlife bandits have been exploiting kids since the beginning of time. At least as far back as Dickens." He frowned and rose. "Speaking of bandits, what's that dog raising hell about?"

As Luke and Will let themselves out into the shadow of the porch, Ash flipped on his front floodlight. The old man shouted from his chair in the door and brought the dog, tail down, back to the porch. A chestnut horse, its ears laid back from nervousness, danced in the gleam of the flood. Amie Roberts, looking no more substantial than a paper doll, swung from the saddle, spoke to her horse, then ran toward Ash with both hands out in greeting. Luke watched her bend to an embrace just as Nan used to do, and his throat closed on him.

"That old man should have had a house full of kids," Will said. "Him and Nan both. Want to go over?"

114

When Luke shook his head, Will turned back into the house. "No disrespect intended to your coffee, Luke, but why don't we wash it away with some of that wine?"

As Luke filled their glasses, his mind went back to Will's words. Cryptic. What did it all add up to? "Then you think maybe Tom was hit on the head because of something Roberts had put him up to?"

"It's a distinct possibility. Or maybe the money, like the sheriff thinks. Remember, somebody tore up Tom's cabin looking for something."

"Your mother brought a bundle of something, probably papers, here for Ash to hide the night of Tom's funeral. Maybe that was what they wanted."

Will shook his head. "That was some stuff that was special to her. When she fretted about it to me, I told her to go ahead, make herself comfortable about it." He didn't smile, but like Nan, his eyes changed when he was amused. "Any papers they might have wanted were with me," he said. "But they wouldn't know that, would they?"

Bandit began again, whining this time. From the doorway they watched Amie Roberts walk stiffly away from Ash's cabin, mount her horse, and gallop off toward the road.

"I give Ash two minutes to ring that bell," Will said. "If you don't mind, I'll stretch out here on this sofa."

"What about supper?"

Will shook his head. "No food, thanks." He was already down, eyes closed and his arms folded over his chest. "Like good intentions, coffee sometimes works the opposite of how I think it will." He opened one eye and looked at Luke. "Don't get upset if I'm not here when you get back. I won't be gone long, and I'll stay in touch."

Ash rang his bell from the porch almost at once.

"I thought you had taken off," he said as Luke worked his way past Bandit's tongue.

"You had company," Luke reminded him. "Far be it from me to crash in. Have you thought about dinner?"

"There's bread and cheese and canned soup. Will that hold you?"

"I'm about as hungry as you are," Luke reminded him. Ash wheeled back and forth silently, setting things out of the refrigerator. "That poor kid was near hysterical," he finally offered.

Luke turned to stare at him. "About Nan?"

"In a cross-country way," Ash replied. "She kept losing control and crying so much it was hard to know what was really getting to her. She said she came because I was friends to Nan as well as to her. She said all the right things, of course, along with a lot of things she probably didn't mean to say. According to her, that forester Bo Sanders who works for her husband was named as one of the men who went to Nan's cabin."

"That whole business about Nan and other men is a lot of bullshit," Luke exploded.

"I was only telling you what Amie was having fits about," Ash said quietly. "Come to think about it, Bo Sanders would make a lot better match for her than what she's got. And she knows it, too."

Luke set the steaming soup bowls on the table and sat down. "So Burt Roberts's young wife is loose in the saddle."

"Burt's gone a lot," Ash said. "Enough for those two young people to form a kind of attachment for each other."

That unaccountable anger rose, painful in Luke's throat. Attachment was one of Ash's pet words . . . the pain of attachment.

"Come on, Ash," he said. "You mean those two

116

young people are in love? What is there about you that you can't bring yourself to pronounce the word love?"

Ash dropped a full slice of generously buttered bread into his soup and began cutting it in careful squares. "A man can say that word only so many times before it starts burning his mouth."

Will was gone when Luke got back to his cabin. The mugs and wineglasses had been washed clean and set to dry on a towel by the sink the way Ash had taught Luke to leave things.

Chapter 9

Except where the ground was soft from rain or unusually rough, Ash Porter stubbornly wheeled himself everywhere. Although the hearing was held in a courtroom with polished wooden floors, Ash signaled Luke to push him down the center aisle. This request was sufficiently distracting that Luke didn't notice Will Harrow on the bench across from them until Ash nodded to him. Will returned the greeting with a nod. He neither met Luke's eyes nor acknowledged his presence.

In his office Eddie Dodge had said he wanted a frame to put the events in. The word could not have been better chosen.

As the child of a beekeeper, Luke understood frames. Given the weight of honey once the supers were filled, each section had to be solidly constructed. Standard wood had to be cut down for the frame to fit exactly on the brood boxes. Only with the wooden tongues glued firmly into their grooves, with nails driven in at each corner, could the builder be certain the frame would hold.

Murder was an enormity that required painstaking workmanship. Nan's death was trimmed from anguish and horror to discrete factors: when the body was found, the location of the tree against which her body rested, the angle at which her nearly severed head lay on her own shoulder. Only the time of death was not precise: "between three-fifteen and three forty-five, approximately." Luke Adams had left Ash Porter's at about three-thirty to meet the victim at the location marked by a tidy X on the diagram. The cause of death was related in medical gibberish that boiled down to her having had her throat cut. The investigator added that since Nan Harrow was an active young woman of known strength and stamina, and since no evidence of a struggle was observable at the site of the crime, it could be presumed that only an assailant known to the victim would have been permitted close enough to commit the crime in question.

If the first side of that frame was opportunity, the second represented means. The murder weapon was displayed, a long, slender steel knife that had been found in the brush a few yards away from Nan Harrow's body.

The wooden handle of the murder knife gave the forensic specialist an opportunity to educate the jury on the intricacies of his specialty. Although the knife handle was clean of fresh prints, it bore a deep protein stain that matched Ash Porter's fingerprints. Fairly recent advances in the field had revealed that human flesh left a protein impression on porous materials. Neither the passage of time nor ordinary attempts to clean the surface could erase this deep stain. Laboratory examination identified the dried blood along the blade as that of the victim, Nan Harrow. The technician pointed out that the Porter prints could have been of long standing and the weapon either wiped clean of fresh prints or wielded by an assailant whose hands were covered.

Associating Luke Adams with that knife was not as simple as the questioner might have desired. Ruby identified the knife as one of a brand she always kept stocked in her general store. "I always stock them," she said. "They take a keener edge than any ordinary knife. A lot of folks up here bring home game to dress. And the price is right. Folks up here also can't throw money away for a collection of knives. They want one tool that will cut a buck deer's throat as easy as it will slice potatoes for soup. But they do have to replace knives a lot; they throw them out with peelings or nip the edges off the blades trying to pry jars open. There must be a hundred of those knives on this mountain, half of them buried in compost heaps."

She turned snappish when asked if Ash Porter had bought any of the knives. "You expect me to remember every piece of cutlery I ring on that register? That's unreasonable." When pressed, she did say it was Ash Porter's custom to rent out his cabin complete with kitchen equipment, and that he generally had to replace a lot of items when the place changed renters. She couldn't remember whether he had bought a knife for the cabin after the last renters, Nan Harrow and her boys, moved out.

Luke himself, when asked if such a knife was currently part of the kitchen equipment in Ash's rental cabin, replied that he didn't know. "I haven't prepared any food there, nothing except coffee. I've eaten all my meals over at Ash's."

He was corrected on that. "Except for the day following Tom Harrow's death, when you and Ash ate in Bardenville, and the meal you ate out with Nan Harrow in Featherton a few days later."

Luke jerked his mind back from the torpor he had fought since wakening. What was this about? Who had kept track of every move he made? Who had seen him with Nan that day in town? More particularly, why had they remembered?

"Then you claim not to recognize this knife that was used to kill Nan Harrow?" Kill was an ice-water word with Nan's blood bubbling through it.

"That knife looks like every kitchen knife I've ever seen in my life. I didn't kill Nan Harrow. What cause would I have? We were friends."

Opportunity had been established, the means was clear, and Luke's own angry question brought up motive. "More than friends, maybe? Maybe you didn't like other people being more than friends with your woman."

"That's a madman's talk."

"A madman who spends a lot of time, day and night, seeing what goes on in the woods."

Although Luke tried to choose his words carefully, his meetings with Nan on the path through the woods came out sounding stealthy and soiled. A restless murmur stirred the room when Luke, his jaws aching with anguish, admitted "carnal knowledge" of Nan Harrow.

The tack changed again so abruptly that Luke, fighting his mind's effort to escape the entire process, could not find a name for the fourth side of the frame.

"Where did you go and what did you do in the hour after you were returned to Ash Porter's cabin under your own recognizance?"

"I poured Ash a Scotch," he said. "Then I went to my cabin across the way, hoping that he'd rest a little, maybe take a nap."

"And what did you do there?"

Luke tried to keep the hesitation from his voice. What was this about? Where was it leading? "I made coffee and drank it."

"You didn't leave the cabin for any reason during that time."

"I did not."

"After Sheriff Dodge dropped you at Ash Porter's door and before he could get to Nan Harrow's cabin, her place was ransacked, just as her son Tom's had been after the fire. Are you prepared to state under oath that you were in your cabin on Porter's land, just drinking coffee, during that time?"

Luke paused, fighting a sudden rise of fury. So even the county attorney realized what a weak motive they had ascribed to him. Why else would he feel impelled to add robbery to brace his case?

To Luke's relief, Will Harrow rose to his feet. "Coffee and then wine," he said. "I know because I was there with him."

Luke avoided Ash's angry stare as he stepped down to permit Will Harrow to come forward.

When asked what time he arrived at Luke's cabin, Will shook his head. "I haven't any idea. When I heard the report of my mother's death, I drove straight up there. It was probably around five. I waited there for Luke Adams and Ash to come home."

"How did you first get word that your mother had been murdered?"

Luke watched Will's unchanging face with fascination. He hadn't thought to ask himself this, but how *had* Will heard about Nan so quickly? Nobody knew Will had been coming and going from Nan's. Whom had he been in contact with on the mountain?

"A man drove into a station where I was buying gas and told the attendant. I used the public phone to call a friend of Mother's and was told it was true."

"Is that friend in this room?"

"Mrs. Jerry Hodges," Will replied. Evie nodded from the back of the room, her eyes on his.

"After hearing this news, you confirmed it, then drove directly to this man's cabin rather than go to your mother?"

Will nodded.

"Can you explain why you went *there*?"

Will spoke slowly. "Because of what I overheard. The talker said Nan Harrow's soldier boyfriend had slit her throat. Where would you have gone?"

Will took the high ground with that challenge. The questions went on, but the tone sounded careful. "You heard that this man murdered your mother, yet you went to his home and waited for him. Didn't you doubt that he might be allowed to return?"

Will shook his head. "I knew he hadn't done it. He had no reason to kill Nan. They were friends."

"Mr. Harrow, as far as we know, you have been absent from the mountain for over two weeks. You failed to appear at the preliminary hearing following your brother's death, and were subsequently absent from his funeral, yet you knew this man well enough to be certain not only that he hadn't killed your mother but that he would be allowed to go free. You must have felt very secure about Luke Adams. When did you first become acquainted with him?"

"I have the same as known him all my life, through Ash Porter."

"Secondhand. When did you first meet?"

"Last night."

"You did not meet this man until *after* you heard he had killed your mother. Now you are offering to supply him with an alibi for the period of time in which your mother's home was invaded?"

"No, sir. I am not offering to supply him with an alibi. I'm telling you I was with Luke Adams from the time he left Ash in his own cabin. I stayed there with him until well after dark. Ash had a caller. Adams waited until Ash was alone again to go home."

"A caller?"

"Yes, sir. Ash had company, and Luke didn't want to intrude."

"Can you give us the name of that caller?"

"That would be secondhand, wouldn't it?" Will turned to the judge. "Your Honor, may I make an observation concerning one troubling statement about my mother's death?"

At the judge's nod, Will hesitated only a moment. "In reference to my mother's knowing her assailant, I have trouble with that. My mother was strong and agile. She was also a small woman, slightly over five foot three and weighing less than a hundred and twenty pounds. I would guess that a woman of that size would offer no problem to a hunter accustomed to stalking and killing full-sized deer."

The attorney did not comment, but turned to his next question. "One thing further before we dismiss you temporarily, Mr. Harrow. Can you explain to the jury why you have been absent from your mother's side during this difficult time following your brother's death?"

Will sat silent momentarily. "What you are asking has nothing to do with this inquiry, but I don't mind telling you. My mother was widowed young. I grew up watching her slow healing from that loss. I was out of the state at the time of my brother's death. My mother begged me not to come home. When I insisted, she relented only if I would stay out of sight and not let anyone know I was here."

"Why?"

"She was frantic with grief for Tom and fear for me. She said too many people had already died and I was all she had left to lose."

The emotional climate in the room shifted in some indefinable way with Will's words, but the frame had been shaped. In spite of Will's obvious support and his statements eliminating the robbery angle, the frame was in place, and Luke was the only one who fit it.

Ash Porter supported Luke's story and named Amie Roberts as the caller who had come to bring him sympathy for his loss of a dear friend. He insisted Luke did not have time to reach the place where Nan was found before the sheriff called. No, he hadn't looked at the clock; he just knew.

Bo Sanders stated that he had gone into that tract of woods on company business. He took the path as a shortcut to a stand of timber Mr. Roberts had particularly asked him to check on. He described finding Nan's body. He hadn't realized for the first moment she was dead. He had spoken to her before he saw the seepage of fresh blood down the front of her shirt. He had turned immediately and run back through the woods to his car to call the sheriff's office. He had not seen any other person in the woods, not Luke Adams, not anyone at all.

Luke looked at the faces of the jury members. All were strangers to him. But they were not strangers to each other. He was an outsider, a double outsider really, being only "the boy Ash Porter had raised up," and a man gone from the mountain too long to be one of them. What had Nan said about the community meetings? That they were only looking for someone to blame? Opportunity, means, motive. Only the identity of the murderer was left to be nailed in.

Luke watched Silas Engel rise to speak and could almost hear the nails being hammered in. To the poorly concealed delight of many of the spectators, Engel insisted again that Nan Harrow had men coming to that cabin of hers at all hours. He stabbed his finger at Luke, at Bo Sanders, and finally at Will Harrow, and would have launched into the Book of Isaiah if he had not been forced to step down.

With the frame a little askew, Bo Sanders was called back to the stand. He said that indeed he had occasionally "stopped by" Nan's cabin to visit with Will Harrow and his mother, of course, when she chanced to be there.

Sanders was followed by Burt Roberts, who was effusively embarrassed not to be able to remember telling Bo Sanders to inspect that tract of woods. "It's been a busy time," he said. "While it is possible I sent him on that particular errand, I pride myself on my good memory. I do know I was rushed to make it to an appointment in the valley, and my head was wholly on that."

When the jury panel filed out for deliberations, Luke rose to take Ash out into the fresh air. Ash pushed him away from the handles of the chair and glared up at him. "You could have told me Will was there last night."

"I didn't know whether he was still hiding out or not," Luke admitted.

"He ought to be," Ash said. "He had no business showing his face around here yet."

The sun was brilliant beyond the open door. When Luke paused there a moment behind the wheelchair, Ash spoke to him roughly. "Turn me around, Luke. I want to go back inside."

Before Luke could protest, the old man began tugging at the wheels, twisting the handle of the chair out of Luke's grip. Luke shrugged and fell into step behind the chair.

Will Harrow still sat on the empty bench. When Ash wheeled across to join him, Will slid down the bench to sit at Ash's side. Neither of them even glanced back at Luke as they talked quietly. Only when the jury began to file back in did Ash return to Luke's side.

The jury found insufficient indication to bring in a true bill. Nan Harrow was declared the victim of homicide by person or persons unknown, pending further investigation.

"Murder," Silas Engel stated in the dead quiet of the room. "Bloody murder."

Ash sat quietly in his chair as the room began to empty. Luke's mental numbness had become physical as well. He heard whispering voices as people passed, and he fought for his breath. The nausea was back. He heard Will slide in beside him but didn't move.

"That was a narrow one," Will said quietly.

126

"It doesn't matter that much," Luke told him. "It doesn't bring back Nan."

Luke wheeled Ash Porter's chair down the ramp that had been installed beside the worn stone steps. With his head bent away from the sun, he didn't see Linden Porter until she stood before them on the sidewalk, blocking their way. She must have already been there when the jury went out. That would explain Ash's frantic retreat back into the courtroom.

He was sure Linden would define her outfit as casual, but the crease of her white trousers would have sliced cheese. Gold bangles nestled at both wrists where she had shoved up the sleeves of her loose-knit red sweater. Dark glasses hid the anger in her eyes that her mouth couldn't conceal.

"I'll take that," she said, reaching for the back of her father's chair.

"You'll do no such thing," Ash replied. "Push on, Luke, before we draw a crowd."

Linden's tongue moistened her lips swiftly, and she took an extra step to fall in beside her father. "I want to know what in hell is going on up here," she told him.

"Who called you?" her father broke in.

"Nobody had to call! The media has been lapping this up and licking their lips since five o'clock yesterday. 'Passion Murder on Wooded Path.' And who gave them the right to call Luke your adopted son? That's not true, and you know it."

"I didn't tell anybody you were my daughter, you can rest easy on that."

Tight-lipped, Linden turned on Luke. "I didn't drive up here to fight with him, Luke. I just want to know what's going on. Two murders in three weeks, and the Porter name linked with both of them. If I had guessed you'd get into a mess the minute you hit this hill, I would never have let you come up here."

"I might have been a little hard to stop," he told her. "As it was, I came in spite of you. And I didn't get into any messes. This place was already at flash point before I came. That garage fire that killed Tom Harrow began before I even got up the hill to Ash's. And no matter what any damned jury says, I would have died myself before I would have hurt Nan Harrow."

"Crime of passion," she said acidly. "What's next? Another death? Another fire?"

"You'd like that, wouldn't you?" Ash broke in. "You'd really like that. Luke is coming home with me to finish out his visit, that's what's next."

"You what?" she asked Luke. "I can't believe you haven't done enough to satisfy even you." The glaze of her glasses gave Luke his own face back, distorted.

"I haven't done a thing, Linden. I tell you, I walked into this. I didn't cause it."

She sighed. "I just wish to God you hadn't come. I told you this was a time warp."

They had reached Luke's car, and he opened the passenger door. Linden looked down at her father with irritation. "Put him into the car, Luke. I want to talk to you."

"I'm staying right here until you leave," Ash told her.

She ignored him. "Okay, Luke." She turned her back to Ash and dropped her voice. Luke doubted that either Ash or any of the people around could catch her furious words. He wondered if he was hearing them right himself. "How about an offer you can't refuse? Leave. Go now. If they ask you to stay, ignore it. You're not under bond, and if they slap one on you, I'll pay it. When you get back to your unit you could simply tell them something came over you. Plead breakdown. Demand a shrink. Just get out of here. How much would it take to make it worth your while?"

"You can't be serious, Linden. Nobody bought my

way up here, and nobody's going to pay me to leave. I'm not a murderer, and they aren't going to convict me for something I didn't do. As for jumping bond, if it came to that, I don't have your fine confidence about making end runs around the law. All of that aside, why is it worth so much to you to get me off this mountain?"

"They're not through. They only blew this one. You're the only real suspect they've got. Ash's prints on that knife pretty well establish it was from your cabin or his."

"There's never been a lock on either of those doors, Linden, and everybody on this mountain knows it."

She turned away, her body stiff with anger. "For God's sake, it's like you to have come up here and get caught in the cross fire of something you don't have a pig's idea about. Once a cocky bastard, always a cocky bastard. And all you had to do was stay away."

"Ash was nearly killed, Linden. Remember?"

She jerked off her glasses, revealing black eyes closed against light even in fury. "Maybe I'll get lucky and you'll be next, Luke Adams."

"Thanks, Linden," he managed to say in spite of the shock waves her words sent through him.

Luke watched her walk away without even a glance back at her father. The old man looked up. He was clearly curious, in spite of his forced, rueful grin. "Whatever you two talked about, it looked like you won." He glanced at the clusters of watchers still hanging along the street. "Puts on a good show, doesn't she? That should give the gossips a little grist for the mill. She had to be pretty mad to drive clear up here and back after all these years."

"Maybe she'll stay with friends," Luke said absently, watching Linden expertly maneuver the sports car out onto the gravel road.

"She hasn't any friends up here," Ash told him. "I know that, whether she does or not."

Chapter 10

"I dread going back home," Ash said as Luke pulled out onto the road. "I dread going home, but I sure as hell don't want to sit in any public place and be stared at. I wish there was someplace to go where there would only be strangers."

"Someplace to eat lunch, you mean?"

"Someplace to *be*. Just to go and be there and not face up to all this. Someplace where nobody knew me and I didn't know them."

Flight. Flight from the pain of attachment.

Linden had suggested flight. Her words were still an astonishment in Luke's mind. "How about an offer you can't refuse? Bolt, Luke. If they slap bond on you, I'll pay it."

Question: Did that girl have any idea how much a bond for murder could run? Or was Porter Properties a printing company specializing in bills of large denomination?

"There's not much point in my talking if you don't listen," Ash went on, looking over at Luke. "What's on your mind?"

"Partly I have been wondering where Will Harrow got off to so fast." It was only half a lie.

Ash straightened in the seat. "Good job, Luke. I needed just one little prod to ready me to face that cabin again. You think maybe he's up there?"

"You know him better than I do. His stuff's in your barn loft, and he said he'd be back."

"That does it. Let's head home." His voice held content. "And I thought of something else we've got to do. You need to go through that book of mine and pick out some shots to take back with you."

"Your bird book?" Luke asked, incredulous. "You have to be kidding. I wouldn't dream of messing up that book, with your records in it and all."

"Hell, I didn't mean you'd get *those* pictures. You pick what you want and we'll get copies made. But you can't wait until the last minute. Those night shots take extra time to make up. None of this twenty-four-hour service business with those."

"Then you've got the negatives?" Luke asked.

Ash looked up at him. "Not only do I have them, but I can put my hands on any one you want. Tom came up with the idea of filing the negatives in behind the blown-up pictures. It was a good one. I've spent half my life looking for old negatives I put in some safe place."

"I already know some of the shots I want," Luke told him.

"The pygmy owl," Ash said contentedly. "You were always crazy about those little things."

Luke laughed. "Crazy to see one," he corrected Ash. "I never saw one outside your bird guide until I saw that shot of Tom's."

The flag was at half-mast again in the circle of the drive at Roberts's place. "I've never seen that flag all the way up," Luke said.

"That's Amie's doing. She put it out there. She had it half-mast for Tom, too, if you remember. And Jerry Hodges."

"When did the weight of evidence against me shift?" Luke asked. "Was it Engel's tirade or Bo Sanders admitting he'd been in and out at Nan's?"

"Who knows?" Ash sounded testy. "It might have been when Burt Roberts did his usual thing of not standing behind his own employee. But Roberts has resented Sanders from the first. It's no wonder Sanders looked other places for friends, like to Will Harrow."

Luke glanced at the old man's profile. Was this just Ash's good try at making him feel better about Sanders's testimony? "Then he and Will really are friends?"

"Have been from the first, ever since Sanders came down here. Roberts never made any pretense of liking Sanders. It surprised me that Roberts even rented him that apartment over the stables to live in."

"But you said that's what he built it for, his assistants to live in."

"So I did," Ash said. "Pull in close to the mailbox and see if we've got our daily quota of junk mail." Luke handed him the stack of brightly colored circulars as the clearing came into view. "Look at that," Ash said, his tone brighter. "I wondered why that Bandit wasn't raising Cain when we drove in. Will *is* home."

Will was sitting on the porch steps with Bandit pressed against him under one arm. As Will rose and walked toward the car, Luke swallowed against the transient nausea that rose without warning. Will walked like Nan, and Nan was dead.

"I'd almost given up on you two," Will said. His voice sounded different. The level tone of his voice that had so impressed Luke the evening before and during the hearing had been replaced by a ragged anger. Will sounded young and undefended, as young as he actually was, Luke realized.

Ash heard it, too. "Got a problem?" he asked, swinging into the chair Will pulled out and set up for him.

"I sure as hell do. How do you go about setting up a funeral?"

Luke stiffened where he stood, but Ash rolled himself

steadily across the clearing, up the ramp, and into the house. "You start the coffee," he called back over his shoulder. "I need to make a phone call before we rustle up some lunch."

Will had come to the kitchen door with the coffee can in his hand when he heard Ash on the phone. He stared at Ash and exploded with a shocked whisper. "Ash . . ." he hissed. "For God's sake, no, Ash."

Ash turned his back and waved his free hand to hush him. "Evie?" he repeated. "We'd like you to come over here if you can get loose of whatever you're doing. Nan's funeral. Will needs your help in getting arrangements made. You worked with Nan on Tom, and things are to be handled exactly the same way, remember? Good! And, Evie, figure on lunch. We're just putting it together."

"Ash," Will howled as the old man replaced the phone.

"I know what I'm doing, boy," Ash said. "Do you?"

Will blew his breath out slowly and turned back to the stove.

Evie Hodges was easy company. Luke kept having to jerk his head back to the table talk. Evie's voice was higher than Nan's and her laughter more open, although nothing like as rich. He had been so slow to admit even to himself that he loved Nan. He knew better now. Love didn't come the way it was advertised. It began with that treasuring curiosity and moved on to this . . . a judging of all other women against that benchmark and finding even the good things about them not measuring up.

When the meal was over Ash suggested that Luke clean up. "I'll give you a hand," he added. "Will and Evie have some tracking around to do."

They had been gone twenty minutes by the time Luke hung the tea towels to dry. Ash wheeled over and pulled down the bird album. "Take this over and look through it," he told Luke. "Just stick a marker in by the pictures you want and we'll figure out which frame it is later."

Luke grinned at him. "You wouldn't be thinking of a nap, would you?"

"Get out of here," Ash told him, grinning.

Luke settled with the book on the daybed for only a moment before remembering. He went through all the kitchen drawers a second time before he gave up. If Ash had supplied the cabin with one of those murderous knives from Ruby's store, it was gone now.

Ash had won two hands of pinochle from Luke, and was beginning to fret, when Will and Evie got back. "I made Evie come in," Will told them from the porch, shifting a grocery sack to one hip to push the door open for her. "I figured you didn't want her going home without supper this late."

"Of course she stays," Ash said. "But you had no call to buy food here."

Will grinned and went through to the kitchen. "I didn't say anything about cooking it, did I? But there's pork chops and canned applesauce in here."

"You can take the applesauce back with you," Ash growled, wheeling toward the kitchen. "You know that pantry's always got the home-canned."

"There are community-meeting signs stuck up everywhere," Evie said during dinner. "I'm worn out on them. Yet I can't seem to justify staying away. Not after Jerry . . ."

"I can justify it," Ash said. "Sound and fury and signifying nothing."

Will looked thoughtful. "Then maybe Luke and I will just go together."

"Why should you, after that charade this morning?"

"*Because* of that charade this morning," Evie told him. "Ash, this mountain is past simmering toward a boil. There's never been so many hotheads looking for something to *do*. The best damper to put on them is to make them look at Luke here side-by-side with Nan's boy."

Ash groaned. "We don't have to do that tonight, do we?"

She leaned to touch his hand. "Not tonight." She chuckled. "Tomorrow night."

Ash sighed. "Luke is going to drive me down to that photo developer in Featherton tomorrow. We should be back in time."

"Has the camera showed up?" Will asked.

"No. My bet is that it was in that car along with the tripod and the lens boxes. But we're going to have some bird pictures copied for Luke to take back with him."

Evie's face paled, and she turned to stare at Luke. "You can't be thinking of leaving Ash!"

"Not until my leave's over." He wished he had a minute alone with her. Panic hit him whenever he realized how the time had gotten away with nothing done about Ash's living arrangements. Ash liked Evie and was close to her. Maybe she could throw some weight in with his arguments to Ash. But he knew better than to say anything with Ash right there.

Will's mind was still on Tom's pictures. "He got really good with that camera," Will said. "Ash, do you know right off which negatives have those good shots of Nan on them? I'd be happy to pay you for a copy of them, little ones I could put in a wallet."

Ash nodded. "I thought about those. I can put my finger right on them for you and Luke here."

With Evie Hodges gone, Ash faded fast. It was clear where his thoughts were when he asked Will where he was staying.

Will grinned at him. "I slept in your barn last night."

135

"Good God," Ash exploded. "And a spare room right in there with a made bed."

"That loft doesn't sleep bad," Luke put in. "I slept there a few times myself, growing up."

Ash ignored him. "Will, you can't be aiming to sleep out there again tonight!"

Will shook his head. "I was figuring on bunking on that daybed in Luke's cabin. I need to get out early, do an errand down in town, and get back for that meeting."

"You heard me say Luke and I were going to Featherton. Want to hitch along, or maybe we can tend to your business for you."

"Some other time, maybe, but thanks anyway," Will replied.

Ash nodded. "Whatever you say. But I still maintain the spare-room bed is a lot softer than that thing in the cabin."

"If you knew what time I plan to leave in the morning, you wouldn't be making that offer."

Ash looked at him a moment, then shrugged. "Your pleasure. Want to take some whiskey over with you? I know you boys will sit late."

"Thanks," Luke told him. "But I'm way ahead of you, Ash. I set in my own stores over there."

Will carried his drink back into Luke's living room and let himself down into the chair facing the window. "Do you mind if we douse that lamp? Nan and I used to like to sit here in the dark and watch the woods come to life. There's always light there if you give it a chance." In the darkness, he went on. "Mrs. Hodges is right, you know. It's not going to be easy for Ash to see you go."

Luke groaned. "That's less than half of it, Will. I don't know how I *can* leave. I came back here for two things: to see for myself that Ash was okay and to talk him into making more sensible living arrangements.

He took my head off the first time I even hinted at it. And to tell you the truth, I haven't had the guts or time to bring it up again. Got any ideas?"

"Nan and I tried all the ideas we could come up with last summer when he insisted on coming back here from the hospital. Like you say, he fires off at the least suggestion that he can't run his own life. Boy, that is one summer I'll never forget. The only good thing that came out of it was that Nan and I ended up even closer than we were when all hell began breaking loose."

"All hell breaking loose?" Luke prodded.

"Ash's accident, for starters. And Tom taking it like he did." He paused. "Luke, you can't conceive how far Ash has come since they sent him home from the hospital. He was a wad. Nothing alive but his eyes, and nothing in them but hate. Nan and I knew he had no business up here, but when he wouldn't listen to reason, what could we do but make it as safe for him as possible? That's when I put in those ramps and moved things around so he had no excuse not to take care of himself."

"You keep mentioning only Nan and yourself. Tom didn't take any part in all this? I would have guessed he'd be as involved as you two. Nan told me the three of you saw the driver who hit Ash the night it happened."

"She told you that? I'm surprised. We never talked about it after that night. Tom had some event at his high school, and we took him down without knowing it was Ash who was hit. We caught a flick. Tom told us about it when we picked him up. You want me to get my own Scotch, or would you rather contribute to the delinquency of a minor again?"

Luke rose, chuckling. "You'll forgive me if I forget what a kid you are on paper. What happened then, that night Ash was hit?"

"Nan barreled her car up this hill like it was a Formula One. I wanted to go back down with her to the hospital, but she told me to stay with Tom. She didn't know when she'd get back anyway." An owl called in the silence, and Luke realized Will had been right. The woods were coming alive with a luminous greenness. You couldn't call it light, but you could see the trees stand apart. And there was no moon.

"Nan hadn't been gone an hour before Tom loaded the camera and tripod over his shoulder and started out the door. The only way I could have kept him home was to fight him. The way he'd looked since hearing about Ash, I didn't have the heart to take him on. I heard him come in and crawl into his bunk about three. Mom didn't make it until midmorning the next day. Ash had lived through surgery; that was the best she could say. When I told her about Tom being out, she just nodded, saying that was probably for the best, that there worse places than the woods on a moonlit night to deal with grief."

Will fell silent. When he spoke again, his voice was tight with fury. "Don't let me have any more Scotch. But dammit, Luke, there's got to be end to this. Just when I think I know what's going on, everything switches. Incidentally, Tom never took a picture that I know of after that night. And he had talent. You've seen those shots. He had real talent."

Luke sighed. "I believe in his talent and I believe he's not to be blamed too much for going to pieces when he saw Ash brought down. Just hearing about it in Germany was like a solid fist in my gut. I keep wanting to tell Ash that Tom's wildness was a part of his loving Ash. That would be a guilt trip to lay on the old man, wouldn't it?

"I tell you, Will, I'm about to choke to death on things I can't say to Ash. This business about him getting off the mountain is the biggest, but I keep running into other black holes in our communication. I never tried to lie to Ash, because he could see right through me. We were close, I mean close. It was as if he even guessed the private misery Linden put me through and tried to make it up to me. Finding out that Linden had been having that affair with Burt Roberts changed the way I see her. Even today when she made that scene in town I kept thinking how tough it must have been for a mountain girl in love to be thrown out for a city beauty like Amie.

"And money, Will. Ash made his pile back before inflation. How does he live? I've checked with the army. I could make him a dependent, but do I dare ask him?"

"That's one you don't have to worry about," Will said, rising. "I don't know where Nan lucked onto him, but the lawyer she got to represent Ash in the insurance hearing didn't pull any punches. The insurance company settled with Ash in something that had six figures. Ash has more money than anybody I know on this mountain and gets less pleasure out of it. Maybe Burt Roberts is worth more. He'd be the only one."

"There's another man who must not be getting too much pleasure out of his money these days," Luke said.

"You mean Bo Sanders?" Will asked.

Nodding, Luke flipped on the lamp to pull a pillow and blanket off the shelf for Will.

"Bo just walked into a vacuum with that girl," Will told him. "If it hadn't been him, it would have been another young guy who knew how to be tender." He paused. "And just for the record, Luke. It *was* me that Bo Sanders came to the cabin to see." He spread the blanket to lap over as a top sheet and tossed the pillow at the end of the daybed. "When you hear me splashing around in the morning, just turn over. I really have to be out of here like a shot."

Even if Will hadn't disappeared into the john as he spoke, Luke knew he wouldn't have had the guts to ask him what the business was. Nor had he had been able to ask about Nan's funeral.

Chapter 11

The smell of fresh coffee greeted Luke on the porch. "Come in, come in," Ash called. When Luke made it past Bandit to get inside, Ash nodded with approval to see the bird album under his arm. "Good. I was afraid you'd forget to bring that. Pour yourself some coffee while I see what you picked out to take with you."

"No breakfast?" Luke asked, bringing the pot back to refill Ash's mug.

"We'll stop on the road," Ash said. "I don't often get an excuse to eat three whole meals out in a row. You only got six markers in here."

"Those are the birds I remember best," Luke told him. "Or the ones whose songs I know. Did you remember about the pictures of Nan?"

Ash nodded at an envelope he had pulled out from behind one of the pictures in the album and laid on the table. The legend on the envelope was in Ash's firm hand. It read: "March, 1984. (Orioles. Ruby throats. Nan.)" "All of the pages you marked are daytime color shots except this one. I thought you were so gone on owls."

"I am," Luke said. "That last one there is my favorite among the owl shots."

"The last one," Ash echoed. "That's the last roll

Tom ever took. He brought me this picture along with some others that weren't worth saving when I was still in the hospital. He lost most of that roll of film, but this one good shot made up for all the ones that didn't come out." He studied the owl's eerily intimate expression in the enlarged photo. "Night photography is an exercise in patience. I don't know how long that boy had to wait for some of these shots, especially when there was little or no moon. Sometimes he got ghosts when the bird moved or left before the exposure was long enough." He slipped a rubber band around the packet of envelopes and turned brisk. "Drink up and rinse these mugs out. We've got a full day ahead."

The air was fresh and the sky clear. Smoke from slash piles punctuated the mountain slopes in both directions. Luke could almost guess how long each one had been burning by the size of the wavering plumes rising into the cloudless sky. "If this sun keeps up and we don't get another rain, they'll have to quit this burning for a while," Ash commented. "But I sure like that smell of wood smoke carried on the wind. That's autumn."

If breakfast was a disappointment, Ash didn't mention it. Luke wasn't one to look a gift rasher of bacon in the mouth, but if Ash's biscuits had ever come out that grainy, he would have fed them to Bandit.

The manager of the photo lab was a lean man in his fifties named Patton. After acknowledging Luke, he turned to Ash without standing back on ceremony. "What a shock to hear about Tom Harrow. He's been on my mind ever since. That's a real loss, to the field as well as you and his family. And now his mother." He shook his head. "I don't see many youngsters with his natural sense of design."

Ash nodded. "I've brought some of his negatives to have copies made for my son. I think they're all marked."

Patton checked the numbers on the negatives against Ash's list, nodding. When he came to the last set of negatives, the black-and-white strip that included the owl picture Luke wanted, he frowned. "This isn't my work. I haven't seen this film before."

"You sure?" Ash asked. "I thought Tom brought all the film to you."

"I'm positive." Patton flipped over the negative folder. "See? This was processed by a lab in Sacramento."

Ash nodded. "Who knows what the boy was thinking about? He brought me these when I was still in the hospital. There weren't but a couple of good shots on the roll. You might try developing anything that looks clear to you. That fellow in Sacramento might not have your knack."

Patton slid the small envelopes into a folder and wrote the order. "Will you be in to pick these up, Mr. Porter? If not, I can mail them out with the bill enclosed."

"That's a good plan," Ash said. "We don't get up and down this hill as often as Tom did."

By noon Luke realized Ash had been serious about this being a full day. After leaving the negatives with Patton, Ash directed him to the bank.

"I'd like you to meet my son, Luke Adams," he told the cashier. "He's come in to sign some cards." At the cashier's puzzled glance, Ash turned haughty. "You'll find his name on both this lock box and these accounts. I had to set them up without his signature because he was in the army overseas. You people have had a power of attorney on file from me in case Luke didn't get to come home before he needed access to this stuff. Check with your bank president. He was the one who suggested I set things up this way."

Alone with Ash, Luke protested. "This is crazy, Ash.

I'm so far away. Linden is only a few hours away, and she's your *real* daughter."

"You get to be a daughter by daughtering," Ash snapped. "This is my business, and a man has a right to run his own business. Do you want to look at anything in that lock box?"

"Me? Look at your business?" Luke asked, grinning in spite of himself.

Ash ducked his head, knowing he'd asked for that. "The negatives of those pictures of your mom are in there, if you ever want new prints."

Luke nodded. He didn't even know where the old prints were anymore. A man doesn't keep black-and-white shadows of a forgotten face.

Ash knew a place where they served giant beef ribs that had to be fought off the bone through a sauce that Luke was sure was going to leave third-degree burns around his mouth. "If you think I'm going to eat again today after this, you think again," Luke warned him.

"You'll eat," Ash told him. "No problem there."

Luke hadn't walked that many sidewalk miles since his last leave in Europe. Every old building, every corner they turned, had its own story, and Ash knew them all. The last stop was the county museum, where Ash showed him the name Porter on a gold claim from 1850 and waterproof baskets woven by the Maidu Indians from Ash's mountain. As he wheeled from exhibit to exhibit, Ash talked with pride of the Porters behind him: his grandfather, who had been a prospector, his father, who had worn out on gold and turned to lumbering. That ranch above Madrone wove through every story he told. It was midafternoon when he wheeled himself out onto the street. There, among the traffic noises, he looked up at Luke. "A man is privileged to be born to land, Luke. With it comes his privilege to die there, if he so chooses. Does that help you at all with what's bothering you?"

Luke studied the old man's face, those clear blue eyes steady on his own. There was no more expression in Ash's face than there was pleading. He was asking to be understood, a small enough favor. When Luke could not answer at once, Ash tried to help. "Is it fear for me, son?"

Luke nodded.

"The worst that can happen is death, Luke, and that's been coming at me all my life. Death can't come ugly enough or slow enough to balance what I've already taken in joy."

Luke dropped his eyes, and Ash groped for his hand. "That being understood between us, let's go eat."

Ash was right about Luke's eating again. He wasn't sure he ordered the meal for his stomach or to have an excuse to get off his feet for a half hour.

Even if the sun had not been poised just above the line of the horizon, Luke would have known it was late afternoon. At the scaling station, lumber trucks waited in line almost out to the highway pull-off. "Those drivers must hate being backed up like that when they're this close to being through for the day," Luke commented.

"They're in there and out in a whip if they have a proper receipt," Ash said. "Sometimes with improper receipts," he added, almost under his breath.

"What does that mean?"

Ash shrugged. "You got any idea how many millions of dollars' worth of lumber are ripped off federal land every year by thieves carrying hokey private-land receipts?" He shook his head, as if annoyed by his own words. "Let's not spoil a good day talking about bandits and low-downs."

The sky exploded with color at their backs as Luke

wound up the mountain road toward Madrone. A lumber truck on its last lap of the day thundered past, leaving the car wagging in its wake. Ash straightened suddenly in his seat, straining to see up ahead. "Look at that one," he said, drawing Luke's attention to a mass of billowing smoke rising over the trees. "I can't think of any tract up this road that's been lumbered this summer." As they watched, the smoke continued to swell above the trees dead ahead, doubling in on itself like bread dough being kneaded.

"Luke." Ash's voice quavered. "There *haven't* been any tracts lumbered up there. Step on the gas. That's up by home."

Cars were lined up at the Madrone turnoff, their left-turn blinker lights signaling intent to go east up the mountain. When they reached the general store, Ruby, with two or three other people, stood out in front, staring up at the widening cloud of smoke. Since too many cars were following for Luke to pause, he pulled into a drive across the road and jumped out of the car.

"Ruby," he shouted. "Where's the fire?"

Her first reply was drowned out by the lugging of the pickup truck that had tailgated Luke since the Madrone turn. She cupped her hands around her mouth and tried again. "The stables," she shouted. "Up at Roberts's place."

Ash sank back in the seat with a groan.

"What do you want me to do?" Luke asked. The question was automatic, but he knew the answer. Mountain men stopped for fires. They stopped and pitched in. That's why shovels always rode in the backs of pickup trucks.

Ash's answer caught Luke off guard. "Just wait right here until that crowd of gawkers gets by," he said. "Then let's go home, son. Just take me on home."

Getting past the fire at Burt Roberts's place wasn't

145

an easy task. By inching along the shoulder on his left, Luke finally maneuvered past the crowd of cars and trucks along the road. He didn't need to look to know what was going on. Over the crackling of the painted stables and the shouts of the fire fighters rose the screams of trapped horses and the hammering of their hooves against that flaming prison. Ash whimpered, cringing in his seat. "Jesus," he whispered aloud to himself.

Luke watched Ash warily the rest of the way home. "You all right?" he asked finally. He got only a numb nod and the quick pressure of the old man's hand on his arm.

The house was dark. Ash waited for Luke to come around and set up his chair and help him into it. Bandit whined and twisted in an ecstasy of relief around the chair as Luke pushed Ash up onto the porch and into the house. "Get the light on," Ash told him. "Get the light on and pull shut those drapes."

When Ash was under pressure, he always went to his birds. When he reached his table, his hand strayed to the binoculars, lifted them, then pushed them away again. The sudden pealing of the phone startled Luke. He reached for it to forestall the second ring.

"Let it ring," Ash said. "Who needs any more bad news?" Luke, with his hand resting on the phone, waited for Ash to tire of the stubborn repetitive jangling. "Okay," Ash said at last. "They win."

"They" was Evie Hodges, her tone wavering toward hysteria, her voice distorted by tears. Luke handed the phone to Ash with reluctance. The old man needed that right now; that was what he *really* needed.

It was easy enough to guess the other side of that conversation from Ash's words. Luke got Bandit's food and filled his dish on the porch against the background of Ash's efforts to calm Evie down. He poured Ash a drink and set it on the table beside him.

"Now quit that crying and get a hold on yourself," Ash repeated. "That's better. We just drove by there and saw the fire. It looked like the whole stable end was going with the apartment and all. The house didn't look hurt yet, but the fire's a long way from over." Ash paused, and his tone changed. "What's that, Evie? My god, woman, why didn't you tell me that right off? Of course I care about Amie's horses, but Will is different."

Luke looked the question and Ash nodded at him. "Thanks, Evie. Sure I understand. I need to get off and tell Luke. Okay, then, we'll see you."

"What's this about Will?" Luke asked.

Ash shook his head. "Evie is full out of control. Will called her about six when he couldn't reach us and asked her to pass on his message. Instead, she carried on about that Roberts fire for five minutes before telling me."

"Telling you what?"

"That Will wasn't going to make it to this community meeting but we should get ourselves down there anyway."

"He didn't say where he was going to be?"

"You know Will," Ash said. He turned away and stared at the closed drapes. "What else she told me is that Bo Sanders is missing."

"Missing?"

Ash nodded. "Nobody seems to know whether he was in his apartment when the bomb went off or not. They haven't been able to get in there to find out. They had to use force to keep that poor little Amie from trying to get in there to her horses. She's with a doctor now. Shock, I guess."

"Okay, Ash," Luke said, fighting angry impatience. "Give me the whole story Evie told, and give it straight. Bomb?"

Ash spread his hands and shrugged. "All this is

147

secondhand, but somebody was passing just as the end of that stable exploded, shooting the roof sky-high and flattening the walls in. Then the fire started, a tower of flame shooting up. Whoever it was had his car thrown off the road into the ditch by the impact. They said it had to be more than one of those bottle bombs that we've had up here this summer."

"And Bo Sanders could have been trapped in there?" Luke asked. "Where is Burt all this time?"

"Away," Ash reported. "He wasn't due to get back until tomorrow sometime, but the state patrol managed to get in touch with him down in Sacramento. He's on his way home."

Luke stared at him thoughtfully. He had only seen Amie with her husband and Bo, and that one evening she had come to see Ash. "Does Amie have friends?" Luke asked. "Who's with her? She can't be there in that house with the fire still out of control."

Ash stared at him. "By God, you're right. Hand me that phone." He dialed and frowned and dialed again. "Trust Evie to be hanging on that line when I need to reach her." He dialed again, asked Evie the terse question, thanked her, and hung up.

"Ruby's," he said. "They must have taken her down there right after we passed. Doc Meyers wouldn't go near the fire, and I can't say I blame him. Furthermore, Will could have wasted his breath. They can't be thinking of holding any meeting down there tonight."

"Will went to a lot of trouble getting that message to us."

"If you go, you do it by yourself," Ash told him. "I'm not leaving this place. I may *never* leave this place again, the way things are going on out there."

Luke was barely out of the door before Bandit took a flying leap off the porch and bolted down the driveway in full cry. Before Luke could yell him back, Eddie Dodge's cruiser pulled up in front of the house. He must have driven straight there from the fire. His clothes and hair were plastered with soot. Even under the smoke stains, his flesh looked gray. Luke ordered Bandit back to the porch and went up to the car.

"Ash inside?" he asked.

At Luke's nod, he reached over and shoved open the passenger door. "Good! I wanted to talk to you alone. Sit in."

Luke looked at him, unable to see the old Eddie Dodge he had traded blood with as a kid. This was a very old young man, harried and exhausted, his broad face rumpled with conflict. "Is this official?"

Eddie shook his head. "Personal."

Luke slid in. The radio was turned down to only a vibrating rattle in the car's throat. "You look like hell," he told Eddie.

"That's where I just been. The only two horses they saved were a mare and her foal off in a special stall in the old barn."

"Sanders?"

Eddie groaned. "They can't be sure until the ashes cool down." He shook his head and then didn't seem to be able to stop. Then, jerking himself under control, he drew in a hard breath and blew it out fast. "Roberts pulled in just as I took off. He was blazing, screaming like a madman, threatening to sue me and the state of California and to see your head on a pike."

"My head? Good God, Eddie. I was off in the valley all day with Ash. You want alibis? I can give you a guy who runs a photo lab, a bank cashier, and a woman at the museum down there who knows Ash by his first name."

Eddie was shaking his head again. "Right off we knew this wasn't any beer bottle full of gas with a rag in it. From what the lab men have dragged out of the ashes down there by Sanders's apartment, this was a real bomb, a time bomb set for the hour Sanders would be back in his own place with the office closed. You told me after the Boniface burning that any mountain kid could hot-wire a car. There aren't very many who don't understand explosives either, but only a guy with special training can rig something like that baby that blew this afternoon. You got any such special training?"

Luke sighed. "What did you do, check me out with the army?"

Eddie nodded. "Right after Tom died. Burt Roberts recognized you there at the fire. He mentioned you'd been known as a hothead, and wondered what you'd been up to. Like, was it really the army?"

"Nice guy, Roberts. I guess you told him I was army all right, and in Ordnance."

"He was getting on my case. I was establishing that you were on the level about being on leave. He picked it up from there this evening, pointing out that a guy couldn't be very good at detonating bombs unless he knew how to put them together."

"You said this call was personal."

"It is. It struck me that you and Ash might take it into your heads to go to that meeting tonight . . ."

"You mean it's still on? I was going to drive down to see, but to be honest, I figured the fire might have knocked that into a hat."

"No way. But, man to man, I don't want you to go. For my hide as well as yours. There's only me, Luke, and every man on this hill is armed. We haven't had a lynching since Gold Rush days, and I'm not looking to have one now."

"Lynching! Good Lord, Eddie. Everybody on this mountain has gone bonkers. What possible reason would I have to blow up Roberts's barn?"

"Sanders."

"Sanders? I never said two words to the man."

"You've got to have figured out the only reason they didn't hold you for Nan's murder was Sanders's admitting that he'd been frequenting her cabin, too. And the grand jury can convene and throw that decision over anytime they please."

"Sanders is Will Harrow's friend, Eddie. That's why he went there."

"Then why was he so sly about it? You saw Roberts's face when Sanders made that statement. Anyway, what does an educated forester like Sanders have in common with a tight-mouthed mountain kid like Will?"

"Boy, you haven't changed as much as I thought, Dodge. How about Roberts himself? Doesn't he have eyes in his head? Can't he see what's going on between Sanders and his wife?"

"You didn't make any secret of what was happening between you and Nan. Unlike you and Nan, Bo and Amie have been careful."

"You know it's true."

"That bunch of hotheads down there doesn't care diddley what I think. It's what *they* think that could blow things out of my control." His voice turned whining. "Come on, Adams. Your leave *has* to be almost up. Why don't you just get off this mountain and go back where you came from?"

"You and Linden Porter. That's what she told me to do."

"There's a first time for everything. For once, she and I are seeing eye-to-eye."

Chapter 12

Luke let himself back into Ash's cabin to find the living room empty. At the sound of the door closing, Ash called from the bedroom beyond. "Who's there? Speak up!" A new thread of belligerent panic wove through Ash's voice.

"It's me, Ash," he called. "Are you okay?"

"Hasn't a man got a right to crawl into his own bed if he's a mind to?" Ash challenged him. "I'd have thought you were halfway to Madrone by now."

"Changed my mind about going," Luke told him. "Did you feed Bandit?"

"Hell, no." The springs creaked irritably. "I knew I forgot something. And don't half answer me like that. What changed your mind about going to that meeting?"

Luke walked to the doorway and leaned against it to look in. "I didn't come all the way from Germany to tramp around on this mountain by myself." In the amber light of the bedlamp Ash's brow and nose cast bleak shadows and his eyes glistened with tears. "Are you coming down with a cold? You look like hell."

"I *feel* like hell," he snapped. "But colds are for kids. Old folks get pneumonia." His voice flagged, as if he had spent all his energy in that burst of bravado. "It's just some miserable bug." He pawed at his cheek. "A good night's sleep will knock it out of me. But don't forget Bandit!"

Either Bandit was ravenous with hunger or afraid he wouldn't empty his dish before Luke disappeared behind another door. He licked the dish empty, shoved it off the porch with his tongue, then came to lean against Luke on the steps. The wind was rising, evoking chittering complaint from whatever small birds clung in the swaying, restless trees. The sunflowers dipped and bowed, and the face of the moon was laced by swift ropes of darkness.

The coming of storm.

Luke buried his hand in the dog's warm, tangled ruff. Down the hill the ashes of that expensive stable fire would still be glowing, and Eddie Dodge didn't want a lynching on this mountain.

What did Luke himself want? That was simple enough. He wanted Ash feeling his old self—stuffing his pipe with Durham, dealing himself winning pinochle hands, and dropping the level on a bottle of blended Scotch. He had told Ash truthfully that he hadn't come all the way from Germany to tramp on that mountain by himself. His other reasons for coming had been his own, not Ash's. He wanted Ash safe and he wanted him happy. Linden was right, Evie was right, even Eddie Dodge was right. Ash had no business alone here on the mountain in the shape he was in. But Ash was right, too. Death was going to find him anywhere he went. The man had a right to choose that place of meeting.

Luke shepherded his drink as long as he could. He didn't want to risk startling Ash again by going in for a refill. And the last drop of this drink meant another day had passed. Another day Nan hadn't lived to see. Without wanting to, he looked toward that certain opening between the trees where Nan used to come out. What had been driving pain had emptied itself into hollowness. It wasn't that his grief was less agonizing, but rather that his anger was blackening into despair. Somewhere, Will had to be feeling the same.

But where *was* Will?

Will was a strange one, a man with a boy's years who came and went without explanation. Where would he be, this night before his mother's funeral as Ash's bedsprings creaked with restlessness and thunder began to grumble to the north?

The first raindrops fell far apart, large, heavy drops slamming themselves noisily against the earth. Luke dumped his ice on the stairs for Bandit to chase down and eat. By the time he got to the door of his cabin, the drops were falling closer together, a steady drumming downpour, and the northern sky was creased by jagged light.

The "good night's sleep" didn't improve Ash's disposition. He was cross, almost petulant, complaining that something was wrong with his eyes the way they kept running.

"I'll call Dr. Meyers," Luke told him.

"You'll do no such thing. That old fool. He was the one who said I'd never be able to take care of myself again, that I'd be a burden on somebody for the rest of my days."

"You know he didn't say that," Luke contradicted him.

"Not in so many words, but he meant it."

"But he is a doctor."

"Let him go doctor somebody who has confidence in him. I caught this on my own, and I'll get rid of it the same way. It rained all night, didn't it?"

"I didn't stay awake to see," Luke told him, starting for the kitchen. "Want to make a breakfast order or live dangerously?"

"Any boy I raise can cook," Ash reminded him.

154

The woodbox was filled with lengths of incense cedar wood. The smoke smelled like burning pencil shavings. That fragrance combined with coffee and frying bacon filled the house with the essence of a winter morning. When Luke had the meal all ready to serve, Ash still hadn't come out of his room.

"Need a little help?" Luke asked, going to his door.

Ash stirred against his pillows, shaking his head. "I must have dozed off there. Just give me another minute or two. Whatever this bug is, it's mean."

"How about I bring you a tray? You could feel a lot better after eating something."

Ash's face reddened, and he fought himself up onto his elbows. "Just shut that door. I'm coming. I told them when I left that hospital that if I ever got back to having to eat in bed, I'd elect to starve."

When Ash finally wheeled from his room and took his place at the table, his forehead and neck shone from the effort of dressing. He ate heartily. Although the food brought back none of his color, it made him garrulous. He leapfrogged from one topic to another without seeming to expect any response from Luke. He talked about his bees and how fond Madison Ford had been of the rich flavored honey from the plantain blooming. He put in strange unrelated statements before taking on a separate tack. "If a man knew the ends of things he started, he might never begin," he said. Luke fought a sense of rising panic as Ash rambled on. The man was sick, really sick. If Ash's voice had not stayed even and calm, Luke would have sworn the old man was crying. Tears welled steadily in his eyes, gathering in pools against his lower lashes to spill and run unheeded down the ridges of his cheeks. He had to be sick to be carrying on like this! But his words flowed on, whimsically switching from subject to subject. A peregrine falcon had been sighted in the woods a couple of years back. The lumbering in that tract was stopped by government order to protect the falcons' habitat.

Luke watched him covertly, trying to persuade himself that Ash had lapsed into the innocent comfort of talking to himself. And who was to blame him if he did? Look at how many hours he spent alone, trapped on this mountain without any living soul to turn to. Just when Luke decided the old man had even forgotten he was there, Ash squinted up at the Seth Thomas and sighed.

"I'm just not going to be able to make it to the funeral. This business with my eyes is too much to fight. God knows I couldn't pay more tribute to Nan Harrow by being there that I do in my heart anyway. But tell Will to come around after, if he's agreeable." He sighed, and tried to grin up at Luke. "Never mind whether it's agreeable, just tell the boy to come see me. And say it's urgent."

Luke couldn't meet his eyes. "I'll do that," he assured him. "Naturally I wish you were coming along, but I think you're doing the wise thing." He rose. "While I'm cleaning this mess up, you be thinking of what else you want me to do before I take off."

The rain had never really stopped, but wavered between falling in a slow, shining drizzle and pattering in swift, transient gusts. When the kitchen was cleaned, Luke filled the firebox of the stove one more time to keep the damp from the room. "You sure there's nothing more I can do?"

"Just be sure Will gets to me," Ash said. He paused and swiped angrily at his streaming eyes. "You'll need a slicker against that rain. Take mine. I'm sure as hell not going anywhere."

Luke shook his head. "Thanks anyway, Ash. I have a parka over at the cabin."

"And be careful passing those bees," Ash called after

him. "They get cantankerous in weather like this. Take care for yourself, son."

As Luke drove out, Ash was a blurred white smudge behind the window. Nan's funeral. Luke didn't realize how tightly he had clamped his jaws until they began a steady drumming ache that hammered in his head.

The little church was half-filled. The mingled stench of wet leather and steaming wool battled against the fragrance of the flowers on Nan's closed casket. He passed Burt Roberts and Amie next to the aisle at the back. Evie Hodges and Ruby were humped along the front pew beside Will Harrow. Will frowned a question as Luke slid in beside him.

"Ash is sick," Luke whispered. "He wants to see you later. He says it's urgent." He saw the news of Ash's illness nod along the aisle to Ruby, who frowned and stared at him thoughtfully before leaning to whisper to Evie Hodges.

Luke studied the interwoven bas-relief letters on the facade of the pulpit, trying to remember what they stood for. He listened intently for the groan of the pianist's foot pedals during the opening music. At all costs, he must not let himself be conscious of what filled that casket.

The single-fold paper handed to him at the door helped. He read the names of the hymns and where they could be found in the book before turning to the inner sheet. Nancy Spencer Harrow. Born: San Francisco, California, on March 15, 1948. Married to William Harvey Harrow in 1964. Luke felt Will's shoulder tighten beside him as the minister rose and began to talk. What could that man, or any man, say about Nan Harrow that his mind needed to receive? He retreated into the numbness of torpor, a mindless waiting for the end of the end of all this.

The sudden shuffling of feet and stirring of bodies

against rising strains of music brought Luke back from his withdrawal and to his feet simultaneously. He stood behind Will through the handshaking and tears. He heard a wordless sibilance as Evie Hodges and Ruby conferred in whispers. He tried not to watch the passage of the pallbearers along the aisle.

"Tell me about Ash," Will said as the car wound along the road to the cemetery.

"It looks like a severe cold, but it hit fast and hard after we got home last night. He seemed fine all day in town but collapsed when we got home," Luke told him. "His eyes are drowning him, and he got dressed with stubbornness instead of strength."

Will nodded. "Had the fire started at the Roberts stable when you got home?"

At Luke's nod, Will turned to stare out the window. "I have a feeling I know what he wants to see me about. Sooner or later all of this had to get to him."

The woods beyond the cemetery fence glistened with rain. Above the pale yellow of tarweed blossoms and the reddened berries of poison oak, dark clusters of wild grapes hung from vines tangled in the branches of a manzanita.

A canopy had been arranged to cover the second grave in a large plot at the north end of the cemetery. The first grave had not settled yet; nor was a headstone in place. Tom. "A mother watches over her children." Only a handful of people followed the hearse clear out there in the rain.

Luke heard Evie's whispered explanation to Will at his side. "We had lunch ready, Will, Ruby and me. She isn't here because she's taking the food on up to Ash's. That's all right, isn't it?"

"You didn't need to do that," Will murmured.

"People need things to do what they can do."

"But Evie," he protested. "I can't stay. I have things I have to do." He paused, then touched her arm. "You

will understand if I have to leave right off?" She nodded, covering his hand with hers.

The service was short, with the minister's words
muffled and mercifully indistinct. Luke closed his eyes
tightly against the mechanics of burial, against the waves
of pain that battered like the rain hammering against
the canvas canopy above his head.

The screech of brakes beyond the iron fence brought
Luke's head up with a start. He turned to see Ruby's
car shudder to a stop in the middle of the road and
the door burst open. Ruby leaped out. In her haste
she stumbled on the wet gravel and fell to her knees
before dragging herself back up by clinging to the open
car door. All the while she was wailing, a high keen
cry that vibrated in the dense air. She ran awkwardly
toward the canopy with both arms up, her hands flap-
ping in futile, frantic motion. She ran without regard
for the neat paths gardened between the graves. Instead
she plunged awkwardly across the sodden earth, stumbling over grave markers and dodging headstones, her
face twisted in horror. She was within yards of Luke
when her wail found words. "Luke," she cried. "For
the love of God, come. The bees, Luke, the bees."

For the length of a breath he was rooted. Then Will
was dragging him toward Ruby across the giving earth.
No, he heard himself shout silently. No. No.

Then she was close to him, with her hair pasted
down by rain, her eyes wide with shock above a slack
mouth. She gripped his arms fiercely, apparently unconscious of the flow of mingled blood and mud es-
caping through a rent in her stocking. "Dead," she
moaned. "The bees got Ash and he's dead."

Lifting her muddy hands to her face, she began to
tremble wildy. "Dead," she moaned. "Ash Porter is
dead."

Luke tried to speak to her, to protest her hysterical
words. Instead, his breath only produced deep, ago-

nizing sobs. Will seized him by both shoulders, his
hands bracing him, hands like Nan's, square and flat
and strangely childlike. Those hands were icy to Luke's
touch as he gripped them to steady himself on the
spongy earth.

Ash.

Will drove Luke's rented car, leaving his own there
near his mother's grave. Evie followed in Ruby's car
with Ruby, now helplessly weeping beside her. As they
passed Maude's Place in the middle of Madrone, Luke
heard the whine of a siren on the highway road. "CB,"
Will said quietly. "Somebody has reached Dodge on a
CB."

CB. Bo Sanders had run back through the woods to
his car to call in on his CB that Nan Harrow was dead
in the woods with her throat slit. Somebody has reached
Dodge on a CB. Ash.

Eddie Dodge was just stepping out of his cruiser
when Will pulled into the drive. The gas-delivery truck
had stopped at an odd angle, short of the tank holder.
The gas attendant was running toward Dodge, shouting.

When Luke stepped from the car, both men fell
silent, staring at him. Bandit's hoarse, frantic barking
sounded from inside the rental cabin, accompanied by
the steady banging as he hurled his body against the
inside of the door. Ash's wheelchair had rammed the
first beehive, knocking the brood chambers and supers
off the supports. A cloud of furious bees still circled
and dived at Ash's wasted body, which had curled in
on itself like a blasted fetus between the arms of the
chair.

"Do something," Dodge shouted at Luke. "For God's
sake, do something." As he spoke, he backed from a
plume of bees swaying toward him.

Will was faster than Luke getting through the cabin.

He had the first smoker fired and was working on the second when Luke made it to the bee room. "Gear," Will called to him. "Get on some gear."

Luke shook his head. "We'll stay together."

Dodge and the gas man had both taken refuge inside the cruiser, Dodge barking into his radio. Moving slowly in tandem, Will and Luke approached the boiling swarm, layering the air ahead of them with clouds of gray smoke.

Piles of the dead bees circled Ash's chair, a ring of gold on the dark, drenched earth. Luke heard Will curse and stamp as a bee got his ankle. Carefully, still working the smoker with his right hand, Luke tugged at the wheelchair to pull it away. The brakes were set. A shiver of horror stirred the hair along his spine as he released the brake and slowly dragged the chair back up the hill.

"He must have lost control of that thing and it rolled down there," the gas man was saying.

"No," Luke cut in, his voice uneven with fury. "He was sick, too sick to leave that cabin. And look at those gouges cut in the wet ground. He was pushed down there, deliberately pushed. The brake was locked. He must have locked those himself, trying to hold himself back. And Bandit . . . there's no way Ash could have locked that dog up like that; nor would he. Somebody pushed Ash there, letting the bees do their dirty work."

Eddie Dodge stared at him and at the cabin where Bandit's frustration had given way to a mournful howl and sporadic hopeless scratching. Dodge glanced toward Ash's house. "Everything okay up there?"

"I didn't look," Luke said, kneeling beside Ash's chair. He reached toward Ash's staring blue eyes overcome by a terrible wounded tenderness. Dodge's quick admonition stopped him.

"Don't touch him. It's bad enough you had to put your hands on that chair."

161

As Luke straightened and turned to stare at him, he saw the drive filling with cars. As in the woods with Nan, his instinct was to run. Will's hand was firm on his arm. "We'll look at the house," Will told Dodge, turning Luke away from the staring eyes of gapers who were getting out of their cars to approach warily, beyond the still-whirling anger of the bees.

Whoever had ransacked Ash's cabin had been methodical and probably swift. Luke, knowing Ash's fetish for tidiness, could tell immediately where the intruder had searched. Dodge waited in silence, watching Luke's careful progress through each room.

As Luke returned from the kitchen, Dodge draped his handkerchief over his hand to pick up the severed end of the telephone cord from the floor beside Ash's table. A siren sounded from the road. "That'll be the people from the mortuary," Dodge said. "See if you can make me a list of everything that's missing. I'll be right back." He paused in the door, his jowls swelling a little from the tightening of his lips. "Sympathy, Adams," he said. "I know you two were close."

Will had stood stiffly in the door throughout the whole operation. Luke turned to him helplessly. "Tom's cabin, then Nan's, now this. What in the name of God are they looking for?"

"First let's see what they took," Will suggested.

Ruby and Evie Hodges, carrying a basket and a box, appeared, indecisive, in the doorway. "Maybe we should take these to my place?" Ruby suggested.

"How about Luke's cabin?" Will asked. "I thought I might stay here with him tonight."

Ruby looked doubtfully across the clearing. "That's on the other side of them bees." Then, remembering, she began to cry again. "Ash," she said weakly. "Ash Porter."

Luke took the food containers from her and nodded for Will to hold the door. Carefully avoiding the scene

162

at the back of the ambulance, he circled the hives and opened the cabin door. "Down, Bandit. Sit," he hissed as the dog leaped for him. Bandit dropped to the floor with his head between his paws. Once his hands were free, Luke knelt to the dog, whose rib cage swelled and collapsed in painful rhythm under his hands. "Good Bandit. Fine Bandit," he murmured. He broke without warning. He buried his head in the dog's ruff and cried like a child. Only when the ambulance siren began again, warning the crowd back from the road, did he rise, splash his face with water, and go back to Ash's violated cabin.

Will was reciting the list for Eddie to write down. "The Seth Thomas clock was very old and valuable," he told Dodge. "The binoculars." He paused and looked up at the bookshelf. "An album of bird pictures."

Luke, in deference to Dodge, covered his hand to pull open the washstand drawer. "Wallet," he said. "Ash kept it in here."

"Was he in the habit of carrying a lot of money?"

Will shook his head. "He used to, but gave it up after the accident. Mostly he worked on credit and cashed small checks with Ruby."

"Checkbook?" Dodge asked.

Luke looked into the drawer again. "That's gone, too."

"Robbery for sure." Dodge nodded, closing his book. "I need to follow that ambulance down to Featherton. I put a call in for Doc Meyers. Anything gone from your place?" he asked Luke.

"With that dog in there?" Luke asked.

"Somebody had to *put* that dog in there," Dodge reminded him. "Like you said, it wasn't anything Ash could have done for himself."

163

Chapter 13

Evie Hodges knelt in front of the kitchen stove in Luke's cabin. "I guess I don't know how to light this oven," she admitted.

Luke stared at her and the casserole of fried rabbit in her hands. "I don't think anybody wants to eat," he told her. "I couldn't possibly think about eating now."

She looked up at him, her face darkening with annoyance. She tightened her lips, deepening the dimples that flanked her mouth. "Then just don't think about it and *do* it, Luke Adams," she said. "You have to let people do what they can do. This is all Ruby and I can do, and you just better be graceful about it."

He stared down at her a moment, overwhelmed by a rush of affection toward this woman he barely knew. He knelt and lit the oven jet. "You sound just like Ash, you know," he told her.

"Thank you." Her voice came subdued, wavering close to tears. When she rose, she shook herself in a determined way. "By the time that gets warm and the table is set, Ruby will be back."

"Wasn't she just going to take Will down to get his car?"

"And check on her store," Evie replied, taking the cover off a bowl of potato salad garnished with circlets of sliced green pepper. "She left her cousin in charge of things. Think I should start coffee? Will told me twice now that he's not going to be able to linger."

"I can make coffee," Luke told her. What had Ash said only this morning? "Any boy I raise can cook." He practiced breathing evenly for a moment before rinsing out the pot to put it to boil.

Ruby got back first. The cabin air was fragrant with the smell of hot food when she pulled into the drive. She cut a wide circle around the hives to make her way to the door. She thrust a brown paper sack at Luke and nodded briskly. "Dodge is going crazy with the phone out up here. He wants your help in contacting Linden Porter."

Linden. Luke groaned. Ash's daughter hadn't crossed his mind. "I don't have an address," he told Ruby. "Only a number."

"You don't know where she lives?"

He shook his head. "I wrote to her from Germany to a box number in San Fransisco. She wrote back and gave me a number to call when I got into San Francisco. There wasn't any return address on her letter." He fished for his wallet and pulled out a three- by five-inch lined card half filled with numbers. "Dodge may not be able to reach her tonight. I got an answering service the first time I called. She's got her own company, you know."

Ruby's eyebrows rose and fell again without comment. "I'll call this down to him," she said. She hesitated in the door. "The coroner's inquest showed that Ash died as a result of the bee stings all right. Dodge said to tell you we all need to be at that preliminary hearing tomorrow at ten." She caught Luke's steady glance and shrugged. "That's probably because the house was robbed, too. And Dodge told me they still haven't found a trace of that Bo Sanders and nobody's seen him since the fire." Will drove up as she walked toward her car. They were both inside within minutes.

"That was fast," Luke told them. "Come on in, Will. Your coffee's practically poured."

"Fast is right," Ruby said. "I don't know how people lived up here before we got those citizens-band radios. Sometimes I think we have more of those things than we have cars. But they are a godsend to a woman alone. Open that sack I brought you."

The Scotch was Teacher's, Ash's brand. Evie coughed on hers but swallowed it anyway. Ash was alive in the room for Luke as he raised the glass to his lips.

Luke tried for a private moment with Will without success. Will excused himself within the hour. "Funeral business, I guess," Ruby said, clearing away the food.

"Possibly," Evie replied, her eyes on Luke. "You weren't around when Ash and I planned this funeral, were you? If you know about that plot down there, just stop me."

"I don't," Luke said, not sure what she was talking about.

"Ash bought that big cemetery plot, room for six graves, right after he got home from his accident, figuring he would be the first to need it." She stopped a moment before going on. "It was like he saw all this coming. He insisted Nan bury Tom there, and now she's beside her boy." Evie looked up at Luke. "I don't want to talk about this either, Luke, but you needed to know before making other plans." Luke nodded. He did need to know that, and Linden as well.

Ruby left soon after to mind her store. Evie stayed until dusk. She clearly kept hoping Will would get back, but finally gave up on that.

The bees from the broken hive had swarmed in the crook of a dogwood tree a few yards west of Luke's cabin. Luke watched their restless turbulence from the window as the dark sifted into the woods. Ash was not over there in the cabin readying to ring the bell to summon him home. For as long as he could remember, Ash Porter had been the pivot of his life, the solid center around which he had bundled himself, like the swarm hiding their necessary queen deep inside their noisy turmoil.

Nan. Ash. What was left? Linden, who was less than a sister, and Will, who was more than a friend.

Will was twenty. Over and over Luke had to remind himself that Will Harrow was only twenty. Will was twenty, and suddenly, in the space of less than a month, without a family, as alone as Luke himself.

Time slowed to a crawl. He walked through the bleak, ravaged rooms of Ash's house and got food for Bandit. The dog ate mechanically, then returned to his place on the porch. When Will still didn't come, Luke whistled for Bandit and walked the wet, fragrant woods until his pants were drenched to the knee and his boots sodden. He had gone to bed, but not to sleep, when he finally heard Will open the door.

"You aren't going to wake anybody," Luke called to him. "Go on and switch on the light."

"I'm waiting for you to offer me a drink," Will replied as the room flooded with light. He dropped on the daybed as he spoke and sighed heavily. With the drink in his hand, he reached for the light switch. "I got away with that order pretty slick. I'll go for another. Could we just talk in the dark?"

"I've been thinking about you, Will," Luke admitted. "What are you going to do now? Is there more family? Nan must have parents somewhere."

"She had trouble with her folks early," Will said. "She never told me what it was about, never even mentioned them, but she was only sixteen when she married my dad. I always figured those two things fell together." He paused before going on. "Then she was a widow with two sons to raise by the time she was my age."

"How did all of you live?" Luke asked. "Nan didn't work, did she?"

Will shook his head. "My dad was in construction and well-insured. She also got some kind of a pension as well as social security. When I got old enough to think about things like that I figured she moved us up here partly because the living was cheaper. We never went without anything, but she never threw money around either. None of us ever did except Tom, and that was only this past summer." He paused. "What am I going to do? I haven't worked that out in my mind yet. Sooner or later I'll have to leave the mountain, I guess, but there's nowhere I really want to go."

"Anything you really want to do?"

Will was silent a long time. "Go to school, maybe. I was fairly good at school. Have a machine shop of my own. Raise bees." The pause was brief. "Get the bastard that wiped out the three people I cared most about."

There was no answer to that.

With the lamp out, the moon streamed in through windows, tinting the interior of the cabin a pale, eerie green. From the next room Luke knew that Will was still sleepless, too. "What in hell are they looking for?" Luke asked. "Tom's place, then Nan's, now Ash's. What are they looking for?"

"When we know that, we'll know who killed them," Will replied.

Every soul Luke knew in Madrone came to the preliminary hearing. Eddie Dodge, standing with Sheriff Meadows and the county prosecuting attorney, had already stained his shirt with sweat halfway to his waist. For Luke the room was a roll call of mixed memories. Burt Roberts and his stiffly beautiful Amie, Rick Boniface and his wife, Maude from the restaurant, and the gas-delivery man who had been the first to chance on Ash Porter's body. Ruby, of course, and Evie Hodges, who had ridden down the valley together. Will had insisted on bringing his own car.

Then there was Linden Porter.

Linden sat alone on a bench. That was ridiculous. She wasn't sitting alone. How did she manage to create enough personal space around herself to render the family at the end of the bench functionally invisible? She was a study in stylish grief, from her shining hair to those incredible ankles and fine, long feet, all gleaming black. She had to have invested in the linen suit before being notified of Ash's death, but it could have been tailor-made for this appearance. The long-line blazer and flowing pleated skirt completely matched the shaded glasses that hid her eyes. The only relief was a luminous off-white, a narrow satin scarf separating the jacket from her smooth throat, and pearl earrings half hidden under the fall of her hair.

To look at those present was to evoke the missing. Nan, Ash, and, strangely enough, Bo Sanders.

The coroner's report had nothing new to add. Deputy Coroner Dodge had apparently rehearsed his statement. He then called on the officiating physician, Dr. Meyers, who testified that while Ash Porter's face and hands had been stung several hundred times, the number of stings was irrelevant. One or two stings would have caused the physical reactions that killed him, given his established sensitivity to bee venom.

The county attorney had blossomed under the renewed light of publicity. His face was flushed with vigorous color, and Luke decided, judging from the attorney's stalwart posture, that someone had fused a poker to his spinal cord.

The gas-delivery man, having arrived first on the scene, was called first to the stand. His work sheet showed his time of arrival at the Porter ranch at 11:37 A.M. Upon seeing Ash Porter in his wheelchair in the center of that furious "gang of bees," he had stopped his truck and sent out a call for Deputy Sheriff Dodge on his truck radio. He got the sheriff right away, but before Dodge could make it there, Ruby pulled into the drive.

He guessed her arrival as about 11:45. She had started to get out of the car, seen Ash, and scrambled back in, screaming. She was "out the drive and gone" four or five minutes before the deputy arrived.

Luke Adams and Evie Hodges, along with Ruby, had come immediately after Dodge got there.

On the stand Luke separated his mind from everything but the careful recitation of the events of the morning. He and Ash had spent a long, exhausting day in Featherton. Ash had been visibly upset by the fire at the Roberts stable and gone to bed almost immediately after having his supper.

"Did it surprise you that Ash Porter decided not to attend Nan Harrow's funeral, given the long friendship between them?" the attorney asked.

"I was surprised but also relieved," Luke told him. "He was obviously a sick man. His eyes ran constantly, and he was really too weak to leave his bed to dress. Getting to the breakfast table was an act of painful effort."

"No one else saw him in this condition?"

"No one else was there."

"Do you have a theory about how this man, almost too weak to dress, managed to get outside to lose control of his wheelchair and run into that bee colony?"

"It could not possibly have happened that way," Luke told him. "When I tried to pull the chair away from the attacking bees, the brakes were locked. Somebody had to push him down that hill. You could tell that from the deep grooves his wheels had cut in the wet ground."

"You are saying that Ash Porter's death was not an accident, but murder?"

Luke caught his breath. "It had to be that way."

Deputy Dodge was called back to the stand. He corroborated Luke's testimony on the presence of the deep imprints of the wheels. He admitted that the ransacking of the house was suspicious, as well as the fact that Porter's dog had been locked away and the telephone line cut. In spite of all that, it was difficult to justify a conclusion of possible murder. Dodge's own theory was that after the intruder had cut off the phone access and ransacked the cabin, the old man made an attempt to reach the other cabin to use the phone to summon help. The wheelchair could have gotten away from Ash on the slope of land between his house and the bee colonies.

"Your Honor," Luke put in, rising from his seat. "Ash knew the phone in the rental cabin was not in service."

A wave of audible whispered opinions swept the room following these statements. In the midst of that babble Linden Porter rose and asked permission to make a public statement.

The judge studied her a moment. "The court has been informed that you were not present either at Nan Harrow's funeral or at your father's home during the time period in question." He peered at his notes. "My information is that you were contacted in San Francisco by telephone several hours after your father's body was found."

"That's true, Your Honor," she replied. "But in the hours since receiving that call, I have thought of nothing except my father's death and the events leading up to it. Only this morning I have come upon a number of things that could have had a bearing on his tragic end."

At the judge's nod, she took the stand. The arrogant manner Luke remembered had been replaced by an attitude of appealing vulnerability. Academy Award

171

performance, right down to the neatly crossed black silken ankles.

"I would like to state at once that I agree with Luke Adams's opinion that my father was murdered. In a way I even feel responsible." The gavel struck at least three times before she went on. "I should have tried harder to keep this man away from my father."

While the judge warned the crowd in the hearing room to maintain silence, she looked down at her hands in her lap as if she found her testimony painful to give.

"Luke Adams, who was my foster brother, had been away in the army for ten years. In all that time he had not returned even for a single visit. I might add that my father and I had a severe difference of opinion four years ago that alienated us from each other but did not diminish my concern for him.

"My father was involved in a terrible accident this past May. After hearing of my father's accident, Luke indicated his intention to come home. My father requested him by letter not to come. I, too, made every effort to dissuade him. When he insisted on coming anyway, I met with him in San Francisco and tried again to talk him out of it."

The judge leaned forward. "What was your objection to your foster brother's visiting your father?"

Linden bent her head slightly. "My father has never been a genial man. I had been led to understand that he has nourished a seething bitterness since his accident. My foster brother has a long history of being hotheaded and contentious. A lot was going on in the area around Madrone, Your Honor, fires that suggested arson, bombed cars, a great deal of civil unrest. I didn't feel that my father needed a fiery-tempered young man like Luke to encourage his already very public anger." Her pause was heavy with some kind of emotion.

"You may proceed."

"I failed to dissuade him. Before Luke Adams even visited my father, another bombing with a death occurred. Within forty-eight hours Luke's car was seen pulling away from the fired home of Rick Boniface and his family. That was only the first event. He has since been under suspicion in the death of a woman with whom he was having a relationship. I went to the mountain and tried again to persuade him to leave. I even offered him money to go. Apparently it wasn't enough." She sighed and shrugged. "Through all this I had no fear for my father. I think I trusted too much on what I thought was a deep bond between him and his foster son." She turned that lovely, controlled face up to the judge. "I was wrong, sir," she said.

"This morning, with a view to making arrangements for my father's interment, I contacted both his banker and his attorney. To my astonishment, my father had changed his will, leaving the Porter family ranch to Luke Adams. All his bank accounts, his safe-deposit box, and his insurance policies had been made over to Luke Adams as beneficiary. I want to remind you that Luke Adams showed no interest in my father's companionship as long as Ash was living humbly on the proceeds of his life savings and his small cash crops. I would also add that, following my father's accident, a settlement of around a hundred thousand dollars was made on him because of the permanence and extent of his injuries. Through those years when my father scraped on very little, Luke Adams managed to become a first sergeant in the army, not a position that provided him with any grand affluence."

Luke listened in horror. This could not be happening. Linden was cold. Linden was bitter against Ash. But what had inspired this malicious attack?

"I think my father was murdered, and I think the identity of his murderer is perfectly apparent. No one but Luke Adams saw my father the day of the Harrow woman's funeral. No one else saw my father sick or had heard of his illness. It would have been simple enough for this heir to my father's estate, having firmed all the legal transfers, to push Ash into a place where death was inevitable."

She began to cry, seemed to make an effort to control herself, without success, and was excused from the stand.

The room exploded with sound. Without trying to restore order, the judge announced a recess, during which he retired to his chambers with the county sheriff, Deputy Sheriff Dodge, and the county attorney.

Luke felt Will trying to catch his eye, but didn't turn to him. What was the use? Linden had sewed him into a shroud as neatly as if he were already dead.

"Why?" Will whispered urgently.

Luke shook his head. "If I knew that, I could probably get bond set."

Luke's prediction was painfully accurate. The court ordered Luke Adams held without bond on suspicion of complicity in the death of his foster father, Ash Porter, pending further investigation.

Chapter 14

Luke's first visitor in jail was Will Harrow.

Will's eyes, so much like Nan's, were thoughtful on Luke's face. "How much of this did you know?"

"That Linden was a bitch? That was no secret. But I didn't know how conniving and malicious she was."

Will shook his head. "All that about Ash's property."

Luke shook his head. "I knew I was on the bank accounts and the safe-deposit box. Ash dragged me in to sign cards at the bank on those. The will was news to me along with the business about the ranch and the insurance. Why, Will? What prompted him after all this time to disinherit Linden?"

"You didn't see Ash in the humiliation of that hospital. You can't imagine how close he came to death and how he wished for it when he realized the shape he was left in. That daughter of his was an easy drive away all that time, Luke, but she never showed her face. Not once." He hesitated. "She's right about one thing, though. That accident left Ash an angry, bitter man who felt he had a score to settle."

"Are you saying there really *was* a feud between Ash Porter and Burt Roberts's company?"

"It didn't begin as a feud. It was more an investigation." Will grimaced. "I started to fill you in a little bit about all that way back on that night after Nan was murdered. Then I decided I didn't know you well enough. Later, when I *did* know you, things were getting out of hand so fast I figured that anything you knew could only hurt you. In the beginning, I know Nan only thought about it as an investigation. But she and Ash were both on the prod, Nan because of Tom, and Ash because of his own accident and Jerry Hodges's death. I mean, they were on the prod."

"So that's an expression. It means nothing to me right now. Maybe it would help for you to tell me what Nan and Ash actually did in the process of being on the prod." He paused. "And maybe what you did, too."

When Will looked at him, startled, Luke went on. "You can't deny you had a part in it. Nan testified at the hearing that you were out of town on her business and your own. Ash said you were gone on Nan's business and his. Now it must be just *your* business, Will. Doesn't that scare you?"

Will flushed. "I think by the time they realized how deep we were all into it, it was too late." He fell silent as the lawman in charge of the jail clanged into the area and came to stand at Luke's cell door. Luke hadn't appreciated how easy Eddie Dodge had been to deal with until he was handed over to this character.

"Linden Porter wants to talk to you."

"I don't want to talk to her. I have no intention of ever again exchanging two words with her without both a reliable witness present and a recording device."

The man looked at him a moment, then shrugged and turned away.

"She was out there talking to Eddie Dodge when I came in," Will told him. "Sugar had quit melting in her mouth."

"She's got me in jail for murder. What else is she after?"

"She's apparently afraid they will let you out on

176

bond. She told Dodge her attorney was already at work on breaking that will on grounds of Ash's incompetence. She wanted a restraining order to keep you from trespassing on her father's ranch."

"She's crazy," Luke told him. "No court in the world would accept that Ash was incompetent. And anyway, I have to go back up there. That stuff of Nan's is buried up there, and I'm the only one who knows where to find it."

"Maybe you should tell Eddie Dodge that."

"You don't mean he issued that restraining order?"

Will shrugged. "I only heard him tell her that he couldn't arrange anything like that until you were out on bond."

Luke stared at him. "Until . . ." he repeated. "If Linden thinks my getting a bond set is possible, then it's a sure thing. Look, Will, I need a lawyer, if it's only a public defender. I need out of here. I have less than a week left on this leave. I didn't come back here to bury everybody I loved and rot in this jail cell."

Will let Luke's tirade go on until he finally got tired of repeating himself and fell silent.

"Okay, Luke. Never mind the public defender. It would probably be some valley type with enough political ambition to be the county attorney's puppet. But maybe a good lawyer could get a bond hearing and spring you out of here."

"Where's the money coming from for a private attorney?" Luke asked. "You heard Linden. She can probably tie up any resources Ash left me, God help him."

"You forget I'm Nan's heir. Nan wasn't a big spender. So if this takes it all, it takes it. There's only me now anyway."

"I can't let you do that."

Will didn't reply, but stirred and studied the toe of

his boot for a long time. Then he looked up. "What time is it?"

"A little after twelve," Luke told him.

Will stiffened. "I've got to cut out. I wish we hadn't been interrupted, but this may not be the safest place to talk anyway. But now I'm running late. Listen, Luke, you'll hear from me. Cross your fingers we aren't rushing things, but with you penned up in here, I don't see we have any choice. Hang on, you'll hear from me."

"Will," Luke yelled after him. "For God's sake, don't be cryptic. What in hell are you talking about?"

The attendant was at the door and Will was gone.

Until the lunch tray was carried into his cell, Luke thought army cooks were the worst in the world. Most of the other cells along the hall were empty except for the previous night's harvest of drunks and loiterers. By two o'clock, they had all been disposed of somehow. By three he had reached the pacing stage. He had accused Eddie Dodge of learning to be a sheriff by watching cop shows on TV. A fine one he was to poke fun at Eddie! When the door at the end of the hall rattled, he flew to the barred door of his cell like every prisoner he had ever watched at Saturday-afternoon matinees.

For a wonder, this time it was Eddie Dodge and he was alone. When Eddie fitted the key in the lock and swung the door wide, Luke didn't move.

"You didn't let that Will Harrow strip himself broke to make bond for me, did you?" he asked.

Dodge shrugged. "Look who's looking a gift horse in the mouth!" he said. "Come on along with me."

Dodge saluted the jail attendant and tossed the keys on his desk as they passed the outer officer. As they started down the steps, a black Imperial eased into the curb. Eddie Dodge stepped forward, opened the door, and leaned in to speak to the passenger in the back seat. "Sergeant Luke Adams, Mr. Frane." Then he nodded. "Inside, Adams."

Frane. The interior of the car was dark from the smoked windows, but the man who offered his hand was fair-skinned, probably in his sixties, and remarkably bald. His tone was cordial. "Nelson Frane," he said. "This isn't an abduction, Adams. We are a little pressed for time, and this was the most efficient way to fill you in on what is happening. First, let me offer my sincerest sympathy on the loss of your father, Ashton Porter." Had he ever heard Ash's whole name before? Not that he remembered.

When Eddie Dodge's cruiser pulled past the car and paused, the driver eased the big car away from the curb to follow him. Frane's eyes behind rimless glasses were intent on Luke's face.

"Thank you, sir," Luke managed to say. "I'm afraid I don't understand."

Frane nodded and closed both hands on a cane between his knees. "So our mutual friend Will Harrow tells me. First let me assure you that the posting of your bond was not an act of generosity by Larson and Frane. We need you as much as you needed release. Secondly, we are on our way to the local office of the company. Burt Roberts is expecting us. We will be joined by the company's attorney, Adam Bridges. As far as Mr. Roberts knows, this meeting has been set to explore the insurance implications of the stable fire that destroyed the quarters of our company assistant as well as personal property of Mr. and Mrs. Roberts. We have asked Mr. Roberts to have his personal attorney present because of this double involvement." Luke waited. "No questions, Mr. Adams?"

"Two things," Luke said. "Your phrase 'as far as Roberts knows,' and, of course, where do I fit in?"

Frane nodded and thumped the cane lightly on the

floor. "Exactly. Few things come out even in this world, and timing is often vital to success." He glanced at Luke. "My father, who founded this company, was a faller like yours. They knew about timing. I presume I may call you Luke."

At Luke's nod, he went on, staring straight ahead at the back of the driver's neck. "I will begin with the company's concern. Burton Roberts has been manager here for nearly fifteen years. Profits were satisfactory for the first seven, after which a period of diminished profit occurred. Since some other offices showed some parallel figures, due to infestation, fire, or drought, we were slow to pick up on this. However, when the company accounting system was modernized three years ago, computerized if you will, a puzzling pattern became apparent. I won't go into the details, but the name of a single company kept cropping up. The books showed this company making recurrent and regular high bids on salvage sales. An informal audit also showed discrepancies in the number of decks of prime lumber in Olson and Frane's inventory." He waved his hand. "Let us just say that a covert audit has been under way for the better part of this year. In late May of this year, we enlisted Will Harrow to do legwork in our investigation. At the same time, we placed one of our own agents, Bo Sanders, in this office as assistant manager." The old man clearly enjoyed Luke's reaction.

"Spies," Luke said.

"Spies." The old man nodded. "Since you're a mountain man like I am, you realize there are several ways to trap a lumber thief and that most of them take long periods of time. With your father's death and your being stuck in jail, we needed to speed up the process. It was my personal opinion that, as Ashton Porter's son, you would exert a telling effect on this meeting."

The sun was at their backs just as it had been when

he and Ash had driven toward home from Featherton the last time. The driver followed Dodge's cruiser up the mountain, past the turnoff to Madrone. Both cars slowed as they passed Ruby's general store. A blue sedan came out of Ruby's parking area and fell in between them. "Mr. Bridges is bringing both Sanders and Harrow with him."

"Sanders," Luke said. "Then he got out?"

"Sanders was suspicious when Roberts insisted he be reachable in his quarters the night of the stable bombing," Frane explained. "He was with Will that evening."

"I haven't the vaguest idea what you expect of me," Luke said.

Frane's smile was brilliant. "Be yourself, Luke. Just be yourself. This is Bridges's party. You'll like Adam; he grew up in the mountains, too."

The caravan pulled into the circle drive at Roberts's place. The stable area to the right, reduced to a mass of charred timbers and jutting debris, reeked of wet ashes and the stench of rotting animal flesh. The hanging sign decorated with the silhouette of the prancing horse and the single word "AMIE" clanked as the wind rattled its iron chain. A weaving cloud of swifts pipped and swung around the chimneys of the imposing house, still handsome in spite of its smoke-blistered paint.

The driver opened Mr. Frane's door, gave him a hand until he stabilized his cane, and nodded for Luke to follow. Eddie Dodge was instantly at Luke's side, his face carefully unreadable. The dark-haired man with a briefcase, who had to be Adam Bridges, followed with Will and Bo Sanders.

Burt himself answered the door. He stood in the flood of light angling from two elaborate carriage lamps flanking the entrance. With the single word "Welcome!" he managed to convey sincerity, warmth, and an almost boyish vivacity. The word died on his lips as he looked from Nelson Frane to the group behind him.

"I appreciate your making yourself available at such short notice," Mr. Frane replied.

"Look here," Roberts said. "I don't understand, Mr. Frane. I thought we were meeting with our attorneys about the insurance investigation." He looked at his superior in confusion.

"We will have to get to that later," Frane said. "But in the meantime, certain events have made it urgent that we discuss conditions in this territory. Perhaps I was remiss in not notifying you that these other gentleman would join us, but things have moved very swiftly."

Roberts nodded, his face flushed. "This is logical enough for Mr. Bridges and Sanders, but these other people?"

Frane's smile was genial. "It's awkward standing out here making introductions, but I believe you know Luke Adams, Will Harrow, and Deputy Dodge. Forgive me, Mr. Bridges, Sergeant Adams." Luke felt his hand gripped heartily and nodded at the greeting.

"It is all right if we come in, isn't it?" Frane asked pointedly.

The view from the doorway exposed a long formal room on the left. A slight movement by the hearth caught Luke's eye. Amie Roberts stood immobile against the pale drapes that flanked the fireplace. She was wearing something flowing in a fabric as fair as her hair. Her eyes met Luke's and held them a long moment before she turned and disappeared from his view.

Roberts had recovered enough to wave his guests into the wide formal hall. There he hesitated, his face darkening. "See here," he said. "This is completely irregular. We have a simple problem of fire damage. It smacks of invasion of my privacy for all of you to troop in here like this."

"The company office should be adequate, if you

would like to lead us there," Frane said. "But you have another option. We can review the material I came to discuss here in the privacy of this office, or you can elect to come back to Portland with us and do it in the company offices there."

Burt Roberts's eyes moved from Frane's face to Bridges and back. "Very well, gentlemen," he said, his voice low and careful. "Follow me, please. My attorney is waiting in my home office. This way, please."

Roberts's attorney was on his feet as they entered. Avoiding his eyes, Roberts managed the introductions adroitly. Luke only half caught the attorney's name as he watched the performers in this crazy charade. From the moment Roberts opened that front door, tension had begun to shiver the air. Once inside the office, it became almost an audible crackle. But this wasn't tension as Luke understood it. Hell, he was a mountain boy, he could smell a confrontation coming a country mile, but they came open, as flat out as spit in the other man's face. The army wasn't that much different. But this! The controlled cordiality between the principals was somehow more threatening than a man's chest thrust at yours and his fists braced.

Roberts posted himself behind his wide mahogany desk. Maybe that was the same as getting his fists up. "Gentlemen?" he asked.

Frane nodded to Bridges, who took the chair beside him and opened his briefcase. "You used the word 'irregular' about the gentlemen with me. But as we have discussed before, a number of irregular events have transpired in your territory through the past months. Given your long association with the company, we felt a need to air our problems. In the presence of your counsel, of course."

Roberts glanced toward Luke, sitting with Dodge beside him. "It seems irregular that such a discussion involve noncompany personnel."

"I believe their involvement will become apparent," Mr. Frane told him. "Let's get on with this. Mr. Bridges, would you review the pertinent material for us?"

Bridges opened a leather folder and looked up. "I would like to begin by reviewing correspondence from March of this year." After handing a sheet across to Roberts, he went on. "As you know, Larson and Frane has a policy of maintaining the best possible relations in the communities where they own property and maintain regional offices.

"This letter came from an area rancher, Ashton Porter. Although it is not unlike a number of letters we regularly receive from disgruntled local lumberers and environmentalists, we did respond to Mr. Porter, asking for elaboration. Simultaneously, of course, we sent a copy of his letter for your file.

"As you might remember, in his letter Mr. Porter accuses the company lumbermen of marking live trees on federal land as salvage, and having them cut and delivered to a mill as such."

Roberts interrupted. "I don't remember seeing such a letter, but the writer is wrong. No faller would make that mistake. They know a live tree from a dead one."

Bridges nodded. "Mr. Porter pointed that out in his letter, too. He also said that work was so scarce and so few local people had been employed by the company for the past few years that a man with obligations might 'swallow his ethics' and perform the work as ordered."

Luke felt the tension in the room shiver along his spine. Only Bo Sanders seemed oblivious to it. He sat as he had during the hearing on the death of Tom Harrow, staring down at his hands, his expression unreadable.

"Since the territory was undergoing an intensive audit anyway," Bridges went on, "we decided to send a special investigator down here to interview Ashton Porter. Unfortunately, before those arrangements could be made, Mr. Porter sustained serious injuries in an accident involving a truck owned by Larson and Frane."

Roberts glanced at Luke, then nodded. "I know all that and the size of that settlement. A terrible thing, terrible. But what is this about the intensive audit?"

"Routine in a situation when company profits fall below expectations over a considerable period of time."

"We suffered drought," Roberts put in.

Frane nodded. "This was factored into our numbers. In any case, as Bridges said, a special audit over the past four years revealed nothing supporting Mr. Porter's charges of illegal lumbering on federal lands. However, other discrepancies did crop up. A check run on receipts provided to our company trucks at scaling stations revealed that many loads of first-class lumber had come from private property belonging to an investment company in San Francisco. Although the payments to the property owner were made regularly, none of these mill payments could be found on company books."

Roberts moved to protest, but Bridges held up his hand. "Before you go on, the name of this private company, Porter Properties, intrigued us because of our correspondence with Ashton Porter. You had a comment, Burt?"

Roberts glanced at his attorney, then shook his head.

"We decided to contact Ashton Porter again, inviting any information that he could authenticate, to help us clear the company of the charge he was making. His reply came back as soon as he was out of the hospital and at home. He offered all the assistance he could give in stopping what he referred to as the 'rape' of both the forest and the company. He put us in touch with Will Harrow, whom we hired to do Mr. Porter's legwork. Later in the summer Mr. Porter gave us the name of a driver who reported seeing a Larson and Frane company truck, fully loaded with lumber, receive a receipt at a weighing station and drive past the mill where our decks were being set. Out of curiosity, he followed the truck and saw the driver complete a sale at a different mill."

"This is unbelievable!" Roberts said, his eyes bold on Bridges's face.

"And also unprovable," Frane put in. "Before our special investigator, Mr. Sanders, here on site, could interview the truck driver, he was killed by a rigged bomb in his private vehicle."

As Roberts swung in his chair to stare at Sanders, Luke spoke the name. He had no thought of the words being heard. He thought he had only breathed them to himself. But he saw Bo Sanders's eyes raised to his as Mr. Bridges echoed his words aloud.

"That's right, Sergeant Adams. The driver Mr. Porter referred us to was Jeremy Hodges."

Chapter 15

Burt Roberts started to speak, but his attorney touched his arm. "My client does not wish to make any comment on this matter without previous consultation."

Bridges looked at him. "Are you telling me he has no interest in further discussion concerning the company's charges against him?"

"Charges!" Roberts said, only to be silenced by his attorney's glance.

"Charges." Bridges nodded. "We have a warrant to detain Burton Roberts on suspicion of grand theft from the firm of Larson and Frane. Sheriff Dodge is here to accompany him to Featherton."

"Wait a minute. I thought Dodge," Roberts began. "What about Adams? He's on trial for murder."

"Correction," Bridges said. "He's charged with suspicion of murder, pending investigation. He is out on bond supplied by Larson and Frane." At Roberts's expletive, Bridges went on. "It seemed the least we could do, given his late father's helpfulness with our problems up here."

Roberts looked at Eddie Dodge. "He's not taking me anywhere."

"Sorry about that, Burt," Dodge said.

Bridges rose, snapped shut his leather briefcase, and smiled at Will Harrow. "That's it, Will." Still smiling, he shook Luke's hand again. "We will talk later, Adams. My sympathy on your loss."

Bridges walked with a brisk step that bordered on cockiness. With one arm looped lightly around Will's shoulder, he followed Mr. Frane through the foyer and into the last glowing light of day's end.

Luke tagged along, fighting a sense of unreality about the minutes just past. Eddie Dodge's presence and that of Bo Sanders he now understood, and Will, of course, because of Nan, and Ash's, and finally his own. But it still didn't make sense that Larson and Frane had put up bond simply to give him the satisfaction of seeing Burt Roberts arrested for thieving. He had started down the drive when he heard Amie Roberts's low whisper and realized Bo Sanders was no longer walking behind him.

She must have been waiting all that time for Bo to come out. Bundled in a trench coat with a dark scarf knotted over her hair, she had stepped directly in front of him, very stiff, straight and tall, like a proud, injured child. "It wasn't me at all, then," she whispered fiercely. "You were just a spy. You didn't give a damn."

"That's not true," Bo protested. He reached for her, but she stepped swiftly aside. "Listen, Amie. It wasn't the way it looked at all. Let me explain." The other men had reached the cars and turned to look back. Bo leaned toward Amie, his voice harsh with urgency. "Amie, you've got to listen. I can't explain now. But promise me. Promise you'll listen!"

She shook her head, vainly fighting tears. "What scum you are, Sanders, what scum. And dammit, you fooled me completely. You're the same as them, all of them. This was a job to you, wasn't it? Just another, lousy, spooky job with fancy perks thrown in! Look at them! Boy, do you ever fit. They don't give a damn either, not even about all the people he killed. They just care about the money."

"Listen, Amie," he pleaded. "Later."

She lost control and sobbed with her face covered by her hands. "These last two days I died, Bo. I literally died, because I thought you were killed, too. He could have killed you, you know. He tried. But you, you just let me die!"

Wordless rage burst from Roberts's throat as he plunged through the doorway. He moved too swiftly for either Dodge or Sanders, who was caught broadside by the backward swing of Roberts's bent arm. Amie's wail was muffled by Roberts's fury. "Bitch," he shouted. "Shut your filthy mouth!"

Luke lunged automatically. He caught Roberts's arm, tore his hand from Amie's throat, and spun him around. His fist caught Roberts's chin off center, audibly snapping his head back and forcing a grunt of pain from Roberts's throat.

Eddie Dodge had the handcuffs on Roberts before he even started to rise. Amie stood that stiff way, with her face void of expression, as Dodge installed Roberts, his head down at a painful angle, in the back of the cruiser. As Dodge stepped away, Burt's attorney leaned in at the window, talking intensely.

The group sorted itself out automatically. Bridges joined Frane in the Imperial as Will motioned Luke toward the blue sedan, where Bo Sanders had already taken the back seat. As Luke passed Dodge, the sheriff looked at him and grinned. "I knew it, Adams. It was just a matter of time until you got yourself a fight up here."

Will slid in behind the wheel. "Come on, Luke. Let's go." Luke glanced back. Amie Roberts, her hands deep in the pockets of the trench coat, was staring at the ground as she listened to Eddie Dodge. Whatever he said seemed to take a long time. Once in a while she nodded, but it was clear who was doing the talking.

Finally she looked up at him, nodded in a dull, lifeless way, and started back into the house.

"Somebody needs to be with her," Luke objected.

"She'll be okay," Will told him. He shifted the car out of gear to let it drift down to the road. The chimney swifts were either gone or invisible in the darkness, but the smell of death still layered the night air.

Luke had driven to Nan's cabin only with her beside him navigating the twists and turns. So he didn't figure out where Will was taking them until he saw the dark silhouette of the cabin materialize through the trees. Did he want to go into that cabin now that she was gone? "There's Scotch at my place and some leftover food," he told Will.

"This will do fine," Will replied.

Like Ash, Will seemed able to see in the dark. He had crossed the room and lit the lamp before Luke's eyes could find a shape in that dimness. The furniture was standard for a rented cabin—sofa, desk, a couple of tired chairs. But the rug was braided in bright whorls of colored cotton, and the walls decorated with carefully matted photographs of Ash's cabin, Bandit watching warily from his porch, and Nan.

Luke walked to Nan's picture and stared at it a long time. The background screamed spring. A blooming white dogwood glowed in the dark woods behind her, and she was carrying lupines as blue as the patch of sky above the trees. The details could not have been sharper: the curve of her throat at the open neck of a flannel shirt, her wide-set eyes amused at the lens, and her lips making that straight, firm line where they met. "Tom shot this picture?" he asked.

"In the good days," Will replied from the kitchen, where he was clattering a pot of coffee onto the stove. "That's one of the ones Ash ordered us copies of."

That was something else Luke had to do, contact

Patton and get those pictures he and Ash had dropped off. But maybe that was *all* he had to do now that Linden had come back into the picture with her attorney and her threats and her convincing accusations. Luke dropped into the chair facing Nan's picture and saw Bo Sanders watching him.

"You realize I am in shock," Luke told him.

"We all feel a little like that," Sanders replied.

"It's been a long, hot summer," Will said from the doorway. From the glance the two exchanged as Bo nodded, Luke realized how true his own words had been to Eddie Dodge. These men *were* friends, close enough to finish sentences for each other.

"We're still only half done," Bo said. "We have Roberts on embezzlement and grand theft dead to rights. The next step is to nail him for murder. He looked pretty sick, though, didn't he? All set up to talk about insurance, and instead, he's confronted by a man he thought he had killed and the son of a man he had just murdered."

"Nothing was said about attempted murder," Luke pointed out.

"There was a lot of discussion about that," Will put in. "Bridges insisted we wait on any murder accusation until we had enough to be absolutely sure it would stick."

"And Roberts couldn't have murdered Ash," Luke told him. "I thought about that. Burt and Amie were waiting at the church when I got there. There wasn't time."

"That's been one of the big problems, Luke," Will said. "Roberts isn't in this alone. We want not only him but his partner, who's a lot smarter than he is and harder to get a handle on. But it was plain Roberts was disappointed that I wasn't part of the stench that used to be Amie's prize Arabians."

"There are too many jagged edges," Luke said. "Ash

talked a lot about starting things without knowing how they'd end. His letter and subsequent correspondence with Larson and Frane explained that. And it's clear enough why Jerry Hodges had to be shut up before he testified. I still don't see why Tom had to be killed."

"Your friend asks hard questions," Bo told Will, taking the steaming mug of coffee with both hands. "Nan's theory, which has held up almost too well, was that Tom caught at least one very incriminating picture. We had no way of knowing what it was. I was willing to put my money on Tom's having caught Burt shooting the windshield of Madison Ford's truck, sending it into Ash. Roberts is a crack shot and owns the most expensive 30-30 scope rifle around here. But that's guesswork. Tom had to be blackmailing Roberts. The boy wasn't working, but he was spending money like a pusher. Come on, a half-grown kid with a seven-thousand stake hidden away?"

"If Burt had been paying all summer, what made him take the chance of killing the boy?" Luke asked.

Bo attempted an explanation. "Remember, Tom wasn't the first arson case. And none of the others, except for Jerry Hodges, also a murder, made any sense. Empty cars were blown up, flaming rags thrown on porches, that kind of thing. If you wanted to get rid of somebody in a fire that would take his personal possessions with him—say, camera and film—you would do well to establish the arson terror mentality in the community just that way. Then he would be one of a series, not a sore thumb that would scream for motive."

"But Burt was in Maude's," Luke protested.

"In the john at Maude's," Bo corrected him. "I heard him send Amie to the kitchen. Then he said he was going to the john. He *wasn't* back when the garage went off."

"You think he was the running man Boniface saw?" Luke asked.

"You saw Roberts go for Amie tonight. He's fast. And crafty. Whoever borrowed your car to fire the Boniface house was crafty enough to know that memory is a whimsical thing. It might have come back to Boniface any time who that running figure resembled. And you were already set up for it."

Luke saw Will's eyes on him. He wasn't going to ask about Nan, because he couldn't. Will understood that. "You stumbled into involvement in Nan's murder. We're convinced that rap was intended for Bo. Roberts had just figured out what was going on between Amie and Bo, and was out of his mind with fury."

"He lied at that hearing," Bo put in. "He sent me there specifically at a certain time of day, knowing I'd find her body and report it right away." Bo shook his head. "Old Silas Engel walked me right into trouble. Luke, the same testimony that saved you from jail after Nan's murder set me up for the next shot. When Silas pointed me out as one of the men going to the Harrow cabin, Burt knew better than to think I was going to see Nan. He has always been afraid of Will because of Ash, and probably because of Tom, too. That was when our little spy ring began to crumble and Burt set his fancy bomb trap for me. He would have gotten me, too, except for Will's insistence that I not ever be anywhere Burt told me to be."

"You been carrying this around all this time?" Luke asked Will.

"Hey." Will grinned crookedly. "I'm running out of people. I got to be careful. What time is it?"

"I'm watching," Bo told him.

Luke studied Bo's expressionless face. "How long do you figure Roberts has been stealing Larson and Frane blind?" he asked.

"Stealing? About seven years," Bo said. "Stealing blind, about four. It speeded up about the time he married out of his class, about the time Linden Porter left and formed this classy little company of hers. You wouldn't believe her net."

"Why would Burt hang back from murdering Linden, if she was so expensive?"

"The company is convinced she is the brains behind the operation. And she's no dummy. We were halfway through the summer before we got any line at all on Porter Properties. Ash took it hard when Will told him about that company of hers and what we suspected was going on. That was when Ash changed all his property to your name. And look how she took that! But all this time she's smart enough to stay away from the mountain. Nobody knows where she lives. She's got a P.O. box number and a recorder. Period. That's living light on your feet."

Bo checked his watch and rose. He looked down at Luke and half smiled. "Are you up to some late-night excavating? Will is pretty curious about what Nan had you bury on Ash's place."

Luke stared at him. "It's dead black out there and the stuff is buried close to the bees. I'd really rather give them another day to settle down."

"Will is *really* curious," Bo said.

Luke looked from one man to the other and rose. "There are hints and then there are heavy hints," he said. "I guess a man has to earn his bail around here."

"Something like that," Bo said. "I'll see you when you get back."

The woods they passed through filled the car with the scent of mountain misery. That didn't have to mean anything. It didn't take any more than a prowling animal to release the perfume of that weed in the woods.

Bandit didn't move from his rug on the porch when Luke eased the car up the drive at Ash's place. "We should have left this buggy at your cabin and walked over," Luke fretted. "It's one thing to trespass. It's something else to advertise it."

"Who's to see at this time of night?" Will asked.

That was another thing. Why had Bo Sanders been so watchful of the time? Dark was dark and one hour as good as another.

Ash's cabin stood dark and silent in air still musty from the rain. Bandit whined and thumped his tail as Luke approached the porch. Luke petted the dog a minute and then tied him to the post to prevent his following them out and getting stung. Luke and Will circled the house toward the bee room. There was something ceremonial about putting on that bee equipment in the dark. Luke adjusted his gloves while Will lit the smoker.

The hives hummed in the near silence of the woods. Luke paused, undecided. The first hive had still been there when he dug that hole. He had to start all over, pacing off the exact number of steps from where Ash's chair had been lodged the morning before. Will walked beside him, the smoker loose in his hand. Luke braced his foot on a shovel and began to dig. Darkness was a multiplier. Loneliness, grief, and the scrape of a shovel all doubled and tripled in the absence of light.

It had been awkward to dig that first hole in bee equipment; it was just as onerous to dig it again with the earth sodden with rain. At last the shovel went past mud to moist earth. Then it snagged on the wrapping. Luke knelt to brush the earth away. As he pulled the package out of its hiding place and stood up, he heard Linden's voice, low and distinct.

"Hold it there, both of you, right where you are."

Luke felt that same lurching in his belly that he had as a child when she used that tone on him. He gripped the package, feeling that ache of tension start along his jawline.

"Toss it," she said, her voice firm and without emotion. "Right over here where I can reach it."

Luke glanced at Will. Will's eyes strayed to the automatic in her hand, and he nodded to Luke. A wilder instinct than self-preservation surged through Luke. He wanted to test her brittle impatience, to see how long she could hold that muzzle firm.

"Toss it," she repeated. It was one thing to flirt with his own death; he had no right to play with Will's life, too. He sighed and obeyed.

Linden didn't lean for the package but trained her gun steadily on Luke. "I spent the day in Featherton, listening to rube gossip," she said. "That case against you is airtight with no bubbles. I wouldn't have killed Ash if I hadn't been forced to. But it's one thing to take the heat for a little money that no one would have missed except for Burt's carelessness. It's another thing to stand for murder. Ash asked for it anyway. He was the one who kept me from moving in with Burt when that was all it would have taken for us to make a go of it, not only as partners, but as people. But no! He could afford love for every slimy waif that crawled up this mountain, but he couldn't keep his hands off my life. It's going to be a lot easier to kill you, Luke. Maybe even a pleasure."

At Will's shout, Luke dived for the earth as Linden fired. As the bullet streaked past Luke, a rifle shot sounded from Ash's dark doorway. Linden's gun dangled and fell, firing again as it struck the earth. She began to wail, that high, shrieking wail Luke remembered from her childhood fury at him.

Amie stepped from the shadow of the porch, her dead-white face framed by that pale abundance of hair. The rifle on her shoulder held a solid aim on Linden.

"Greedy," Amie said breathlessly. "You and Burt have been nothing but money-mad all this time."

Linden had gripped her wounded arm and was screaming, the sound vibrating and echoing through the clearing. "Greedy, am I?" she shrieked. "What do you know? You always had money. If I hadn't showed your stupid Burt how to make a living in that job, he could never have afforded you."

Amie glanced at Luke, who was struggling to his feet, encumbered by beekeeper's gear. "I'm sorry she almost shot you, Mr. Adams. I really am. Sheriff Dodge was supposed to be here."

As she spoke, Luke saw the cruiser turn in from the road, traveling on feel and parking lights alone. Eddie Dodge was instantly out of the car and running toward them.

Amie stood very still. "My husband's whore was about to shoot Luke and Will," she told Dodge. "I fired first." She said it like a child reciting by rote. She wavered as she spoke. Will dropped the steaming smoker and leaped forward to catch her arm. "Inside," he urged her. "Come inside."

Luke picked up the package Linden had been willing to kill him for. What did Linden think Nan could have given him to hide that was worth the chance she had taken tonight? Dodge, having barked into his car radio and handcuffed Linden into the back seat of the cruiser, walked over.

"You were lucky Amie was quick on the trigger, or Linden would have had you."

"This was all a damned setup," Luke said, staring at him.

"Let's say you gave us an opportunity and we took it," Dodge said. "Burt's been ransacking cabins ever since Tom died looking for the boy's pictures. Why wouldn't they think that was what Ash hid for Nan?"

Luke stared at the package in his hands. "And you don't think so."

"What I thought wasn't important. I just needed to tell Linden that you had buried something for Nan

Harrow. And then be sure you were covered when she ambushed you."

Luke looked at him thoughtfully. "Dammit, Eddie. I have been asking why those cabins were being searched for the last three weeks. Will just said when we knew that, we'd know who the murderer was."

"He was right." Dodge nodded. "What does the name Patton mean to you?"

"The photographer in Featherton?"

"Same." Dodge nodded. Will had come out on Ash's porch to stand, listening. "Patton took a photo order from Ash the day before Ash was killed. Patton hadn't gotten around to processing that film when he heard about Ash's death. He got on the job during that hearing this morning. He was already waiting at the courthouse for the sheriff when we booked you."

"Bird pictures," Luke told him. "And shots of Nan for Will and me."

Dodge nodded. "Real pretty stuff, but what sent Patton flying to the sheriff was the rest of that roll of film with owls on it, night pictures. Ash had told him most of the pictures on that roll didn't take. Ash was wrong. They took, all right, but Tom had been cagey enough to take them to a stranger to develop. Most of them were just moonlight shots, but the second half of the roll were pictures of a man working by the lights of a parked pickup truck, burying a dead body at the base of a slash pile."

Luke couldn't blame Dodge for enjoying his few minutes of triumph.

"Roberts?" Luke pressed him. "You could actually tell it was Burt?"

"Clear enough for a driver's license," Dodge said. "Who do you think the dead man looks to be?"

"Ford," Luke whispered. "It had to be Madison Ford, the night he sideswiped Ash. Will said Tom went

198

out with the camera that night, and he never went again."

"We've cordoned that slash pile over north, the big one, remember? We'll dig it out starting tomorrow."

"How can you know which one to look in?" Luke asked.

"The owl in that picture is framed against Aspen leaves. Those trees aren't common at this level of the slope, but there's a stand right there at the edge of that clearing." He shrugged. "No matter. We'll dig slash piles until we find him. In the meantime, the pictures will do fine."

Lights were probing the drive. Dodge turned. "Tell Amie I'm real sorry I was that few minutes late. But thank her till I can do it for myself." He laughed softly. "Don't tell her I got here late because I slowed down to miss hitting a skunk down the road. She might not appreciate that."

When Luke entered the cabin, carrying the package, Will was in Ash's kitchen making coffee. Amie sat on the sofa across the room as if she were drugged. She was talking to herself out loud, almost incoherently, the way Ash had babbled on that last morning. And like Ash, her eyes flowed unheeded tears.

"I was stupid. I was stupid and distracted. Why didn't I see what he was doing? I knew about that woman of his and the money he sent. But the way he looked whenever she called, hating and cruel, made me feel secure. Then Bo came." The tears overwhelmed her words, and she bent with her head in her lap, weeping.

"Amie," Will told her. "It's all over. What has to be wound up will be dealt with before you know it. And Bo loves you. He didn't mean to. No man ever does. But he loves you."

She lifted her head to look at him. "I want to see Bo."

"You will," he said. "He's over at Nan's now, walking the floor and holding his breath that you'll let him explain." As he spoke, he took the package Luke had carried in from the clearing.

Amie looked at it and then at Will. "After all that, you're not even going to open that package?"

"I know what's in it," Will told her. "It's a bunch of things Nan treasured." He shrugged, smiling a little. "Birth certificates, grade cards, chunks of baby hair from Tom and me."

"That Porter woman was willing to kill for that?"

"She was willing to kill for the pictures of Burt Roberts burying Ford. When Sheriff Dodge told her Luke Adams was out on bond and had something of Nan's buried up here, she jumped to the wrong conclusion. But those pictures were worth the risk of waiting up here for him and Will. She'd already killed her father looking for that bunch of negatives."

"But they prove Burt's guilt, not hers."

"She and Burt have been masterful at covering each other for over a decade. You can just bet that Burt made her a deal. If she could save him from a murder rap, he wouldn't provide the evidence that would nail her on the grand theft charges."

"And she still loves him," Amie added quietly.

Will shrugged. "Now you're into real mysteries."

Eddie Dodge was in the door. "You'll have to make a deposition of what happened out there, Mrs. Roberts." He looked at Luke and frowned. "I've never played tricky games with an accused before, Adams, but this one was out of my depth. When Will told me about that buried stuff up here, we had to use you for bait to get Linden."

"Thanks a lot, Eddie," Luke said. "I happen to know she's a fair shot."

"A chance we had to take," Dodge said. "But there

were two of you and one of her with Amie here covering you both. Having the company get Roberts and Linden Porter for theft wasn't enough. Not after all those lives."

"One thing still bothers me," Luke told him. "Linden will never break like that again. Will her confession out there stand up in court?"

Dodge shrugged. "Maybe so, maybe not. But you know Burt Roberts. He will squeal everything he knows before this is through. Who else has he got to squeal on? And those pictures of Patton's have him dead to right." He paused. "I sure don't mind seeing Linden get hers for killing Ash. That is one icy piece of woman."

Luke nodded. "She's never been easy for me to understand."

Dodge grunted. "I guess that means you think you are. I still don't really understand why you insisted on coming up here at the worst possible time."

"I came because my father told me not to," Luke said. "As he would have told you, I never half learned to obey."

"You mean Ash?" he asked.

"You get to be a father by fathering," Luke told him. "I mean Ash."

The sun blazed in a clear, cloudless sky the day Ash Porter was buried beside Nan Harrow. Amie stood between Bo Sanders and Will while a scrub jay rocked in the woods beyond, drowning out the minister's words.

Just after noon on what would have been the next to the last day of Luke's leave if he had not wired for an extension, Burton Roberts was indicted for the murder of Madison Ford and the attempted murder of Bodin Sanders. Linden Porter was charged with the wrongful death of Ash Porter, her natural father.

"I'll be lucky if this is the last extension I have to ask for," Luke told Will.

Will grinned at him. "The way courts drag these things out, you could be too old to fight by the time this business is settled."

"So I spend a little time on the mountain," Luke told him. "I wouldn't even mind seeing spring come here again. What about you? You're at least as trapped as I am. You've got to testify in that grand theft trial, too."

"Things could be worse. Besides, Frane promised Bo Sanders the manager's job up here when this mess is straightened out. There's more keeping me here than pushing me away."

Luke looked at him. "Same. I'd offer you a rent-free cabin for the two years until my hitch is up. Could you deal with that?"

"I could deal with that," Will told him. "Somebody's got to feed Bandit and take care of Ash's bees."

Luke shook the hand Will offered and forced himself to meet Nan's eyes in that young, bearded face. Ash had been half right. There was pain enough in attachment. But flight wasn't the answer.